MICHAEL GRAVES
PARADE

Also available from STORGY Books:

Exit Earth
Shallow Creek
Hopeful Monsters
You Are Not Alone
This Ragged, Wastrel Thing
Annihilation Radiation

STORGY® BOOKS Ltd.
London, United Kingdom, 2021

First Published in the United States by Chelsea Station Editions in 2015
This paperback edition published by STORGY® Books in 2021

Copyright MICHAEL GRAVES© 2021

STORGY®
London

The characters and events portrayed in this book are fictitious. Any similarity to real persons, living or dead, is coincidental and not intended by the author.

No part of this book may be reproduced, or stored in a retrieval system, or transmitted in any form or by any means, electronic, mechanical, photocopying, recording, or otherwise, without the express permission of the publisher.

Published by STORGY® BOOKS Ltd.
London, United Kingdom, 2021

10 9 8 7 6 5 4 3 2 1

Cover Design by Tomek Dzido

Edited & Typeset by Tomek Dzido

A CIP catalogue record for this title is available from the British Library

Trade Paperback ISBN 978-1-9163258-2-1
eBook ISBN 978-1-9163258-3-8

www.storgy.com

PARADE

MICHAEL GRAVES

For Robert A. Bilodeau, my father-in-law.
You are missed so very much.
In your death, I discovered I was an adult.
I miss being a child sometimes.
Your family loves you fiercely.

> *If God is for us, who can be against us?*
> THE HOLY BIBLE

> *Fame's Boys and Girls, who never die*
> *And are too seldom born –*
> EMILY DICKINSON

> *All literature is gossip.*
> TRUMAN CAPOTE

> *We are all just walking each other home.*
> RAM DASS

CHAPTER ONE
GENESIS

Morning cracks to life. The custard-colored sky douses Reggie Lauderdale. He sleeps, a rosary twined around his neck, his dreams packed with heaves, groans and whaps.

A neck bite.

A scrotum flick.

Inside his slumber, Reggie is making love to Jesus Christ. Tingles boost through him until he spurts like a dropped can of cola. Reggie awakes. Goo warms his briefs.

"*God.*" he pants.

This is the sin Reggie cannot confess. This is the nightmare he has fought since his twelfth year, and now, at nineteen, it still won't cease. He feels dead-ended.

Reggie's mother had always urged prayer. She had taught him to bind his penis with dental floss or burn out the sin by daubing his slit with salt. But nothing works anymore. He knows he must be ill. He knows he must have a condition. A disease, a sickness.

Reggie rises and pokes at his buttery crown of curls. He kneels before the window and weaves both hands together. Reggie prays, "Hail Mary, Full of Grace, the Lord is with thee. Blessed art thou among women, and blessed is the fruit of thy womb, Jesus. Holy Mary, Mother of God, pray for us sinners now, and at the hour of death." Reggie repeats this prayer five times while petting his rosary.

Semen clings to the rubies.

Like always, St. Leos Church begins to call. Bells tinker, the chimes surfing over rooftops, chirping sweetness.

Reggie attempts to smile since, recently, there hasn't been a shooting, a bank heist, a kidnapping, a teenage car wreck, a raping, a terror plot, a killing. Even though Reggie feels blasphemous, he grins. "God … I'm so sorry. Please save me. Help me stop sinning. And please, please don't kill me. God … thank you for one more day, one more Friday. Thank you for taking care of mom in your eternal kingdom. Thank you for dad. Thank you for Cousin Elmer. Thank you for this apartment. Thank you for my job at the church. Thank you for Maria. Thank you for last night's meat loaf. God … thank you … I guess … for everything. Amen."

Later, Reggie crams a pot pie into his mouth, showers, and reads three more pages from the Book of Revelation. After, he adds more scrawls to his list of sins. Next, he dials the telephone. "Hi Jo Jo. Could I make an appointment to see Dr. Dann? For today? I think there's something really, really wrong."

I know this is the genesis of Reggie Lauderdale's truest life.

I see that Elmer Mott has finished painting his lone campaign sign. With bold, blue paint, he has filled in each letter: VOTE 4 ELMER MOTT. Only the L in ELMER is smudged.

Now, Elmer's favorite Parliament cassette bumps. Jitterbugging, he grooves around his bedroom, bareback and crooning.

But the Arcade is calling and he needs a pack of Durels. Plus, there's the gift he has planned for Pinky.

Elmer clicks off the player—grabs an unwashed t-shirt—nabs his keys—heads out. He twinkle-toes down three flights, bursting out to the stoop. Sunrays caress his bare spine with heat.

Mrs. Lolly, in her rocker, bobs on the sidewalk. A bottle of bubbles remains locked between her brown thighs. She plucks out the wand, blows gently and swirly rainbow globes sail down the street. "Mornin' boy. It's an Indian summer! 'Bout time you came out to meet the day."

"Been busy," Elmer says, topped in scrappy hair.

"What? You smokin'? You readin' those dang newspapers? Thinkin' 'bout Pinky, yo sweetheart?"

He jerks with a grin. "She's *not* my sweetheart."

Mrs. Lolly says, "Ya *want* her to be, though. Don't ya?"

"Naw."

"But ya gonna go an' get a present for her like ya always do. Aint ya?"

"Maybe."

"She's yo sweetheart! Don't care *what* ya tell me!"

Elmer says, "It's just your old age, Mrs. L. You're just seeing things that aren't there."

She cackles. "Get on over here so I can give ya a good one."

Elmer shuffles closer and Mrs. Lolly whacks his rear twice.

"I ain't old," she says. "Seventy-three ain't old. And all I see is the truth, boy."

He chuckles.

Mrs. Lolly says, "Pinky called down and said she ain't gettin' no picture on her TV. Just one big box of fuzz."

"I'll make it work."

"Ya do an awful lot for that girl, Elmer. Ya get her all those frozen dinners she likes. Ya get her videos. Ya take her for walks around the block. I don't know what she'd do without'cha."

Elmer scratches his naked gut. "It's nothing."

He always says this. Nothing. Still, I know that Elmer tallies her unclogged drains, her winter-proofed windows. He doesn't forget the pleas, the gestures. Elmer has tried to capture Pinky for three years (even wishing and hoping and praying, secretly, like Reggie).

Mrs. Lolly says, "It's nice that ya take care of that gal. It's just lovely."

Elmer's grin beams wide and goon-like. He pulls on his t-shirt. "You want me to pick up some of that stuff for you?"

"Please, baby. Colace. The store brand. Generic." She puffs out more bubbles. They glide. Bounce. Burst. Wet dots paint the concrete.

Elmer looks up to the third floor and sees the ghost-like girl. Pinky waves, then disappears.

I know that Reggie carries a list of sins in his pocket. He records them several times a day. After his lunch break confessions with Father Fink, Reggie places a perfect check mark beside each sin. Today, he has penned his largest yet. Gazing at his words, he is cloaked in fear.

The List …

A) Getting mad at Elmer.
B) Smelling the front pews after Saturday's wedding.
C) Thinking dad was fat.
D) Saying the A word (because Elmer made me).
E) Getting angry with Vic at the convenience store (it's really NOT his fault they ran out of More Money scratch tickets).
F) Littering on Fourth Street.
G) Laughing when Ms. Prickles fell at the Sunday service.
H) HAVING IMPURE DREAMS AND THOUGHTS ABOUT JESUS CHRIST.

I have read each of Reggie's lists. Yes … yes … I have read every single word.

Al's Arcade, like always, is juiced with buzz. Chic's "Everybody Dance" mingles with video game beeps and pings.

Elmer feeds *The Claw* machine fifty-cent doses. He cranks the joystick round and round. Elmer targets a mint green bunny rabbit. "The Claw's" buzzer drones. Its silver fingers spread, sail down, dive through plushy mounds, clamp, and rise back to the top of the blinking box. Elmer is bunny-less.

"Fuck," he whispers.

Maria saunters over and says, "Are you trying to win me something, honey?"

She is perfumed, shimmery. Lipsticked, wondrous. Maria pulls at her violet tube top which dips low, revealing her flat, boy chest. Stamping her heels, she pouts and peers in at the stuffed animals. "Nobody wins nothin' from this piece of shit. 'Cept you, Elmer."

"I'm *The Claw* champ," he says, screwballing.

"Why's a guy like you need all these teddy bears?"

Elmer dumps in more quarters. Again, he jams the joystick. "These little guys … they ain't for me."

"Who they for, honey?"

He glances away from the machine. For a split-second only. "It's a secret."

"Don't play. I thought you were gonna marry *me*?" she says, her words drenched in titters.

The crane drops again but plucks out nothing.

"Jesus Christ," Elmer says.

Maria knocks on the game's glass wall. "You'll like me when I get some titties, Elmer. I was meant for girl parts. Swear to God."

"I *already* like you, Maria."

"Yeah, but you don't liiiiiike me."

"Maybe I just never told you that I liiiiiike you." He slides in more money, tries again.

"You speak lies." She purses her lips like a shutter-bugged starlet.

Elmer says, "Don't be jealous."

At last, the shiny, metallic fingers pull out his prize.

A koala bear.

"Yes! Fuck yes!"

⁂

Reggie waves to the receptionist.

Jo Jo leans through the fingerprinted Plexiglas window. "Your father came to see Dr. Dann this morning," she says. "For his toe."

"Is he okay?" Reggie asks.

"Yeah. It's just swollen. And he's, like, gained four pounds."

"Really?"

Her frizzed ponytail swings sideways. "He just keeps getting bigger and bigger. You have to talk to him, Reggie."

The waiting room is silent with silver-haired men, browsing through day old newspapers.

"What'cha in for, this time?" Jo Jo asks.
Reggie quickly rises. "Um … an infection. I think."
"Another one? Where *this* time?" She slurs on a lemon sucker.
"See …"
"Let me guess. Okay … on your neck?"
"No …"
"On your earlobe?" She giggles.
"Jo Jo. No …"
"On your knee?" Reggie points to the carpet, toward the devil. "Down there," he whispers.

Jo Jo flushes. She doodles quickly on a pad of paper. "Dr. Dann'll be out soon," she says.

The old men turn their heads like lazy oscillating fans.

Reggie falls back into his seat and begins to flick through the only remaining magazine, *Brides*. He sees garlands and four-tiered chocolate cakes and grooms and jeweled heels and ties and vests and velvet cummerbunds. He flicks from front to back, pretending not to enjoy it.

Ten minutes stagger by.
Jo Jo calls, "Reggie?"
He rises.
"The doc's ready for you."
"Thanks, Jo Jo."

A pane of paper crinkles beneath Reggie. He waits, boxed by walls checked in sailboats. His body shudders.

He prays silently, "God … Please let Dr. Dann fix me up."

I know that Reggie is riled by visions. Candy stripers, needles. Massive blue pills. Death and caskets, eyes finally sewn shut. I am certain that Reggie sees an early ascent to heaven with no chance of the world he has always imagined. The world which has yet to begin.

Dr. Dann lumbers inside the examination room. "Lauderdale," he says.

Reggie smiles weakly. He is pinning down tears.

Dr. Dann snaps off his latex gloves and leans against the wall. "Been runnin' late all day. Mind if I shave while we chat?"

"Oh. *No*. Go ahead."

"Thanks, Reg." He pulls an electric razor from a drawer. Dr. Dann snaps the trimmer to life and it chomps off his stubble. Above the purring, he says, "I told you, you don't have Parkinson's and you don't have scoliosis."

"I know. I believe you."

"You're in here, what, a couple times a month? But I have to tell you, everything's perfectly okay. You're a healthy guy."

Reggie covers his face. "I ... don't think so."

"You're exactly like your mom was."

"She always knew she'd be sick."

"Reg, your mom thought she had everything. She even came in once terrified about polio."

"She also thought she had cancer. And she *did*. And now she's gone."

Dr. Dann kills his waning shaver. "Alright. What's up now?" Reggie says, "See, I wonder if there's, like, a condition ... a condition for ... your privates. Because, I keep having these dreams. They're not ... *nice* dreams. Really sinful. Big sinning in these ones. And then I wake up and there's ..."

"Semen?"

"Um ... yeah." Reggie blanches with hot shame.

"Reg, you had an orgasm."

"I know. I *always* do. I need to make it stop. There's something *wrong*. I'm nineteen. I should be able to control it by now."

"You had a wet dream. It's natural. This happens to every young man. Especially if they don't, you know, release."

"Well, I can't ... *release*. It's wrong. It's bad."

"Ever had a girlfriend?"

"No," Reggie whispers.

"Never?"

"No."

Dr. Dann coughs. He searches through his cabinets, finds some Lectric Shave and slicks his pink flesh. Spice taints the air. "You need to have sex," he finally says.

"That's against my religion."
"You need to masturbate, then."
"That's against my religion too."
"Who told you that, Reggie?"
"My mom. My dad," he says. "My church."
Dr. Dann sighs and opens the door. "I can't help you then."
"I'm sick! I can't dream *anymore*. Please help me. Give me a pill or, I don't know, a shot?"
"I guess the only thing you can do is … pray."

I watch Elmer stake his sign in the balding grass.

I watch Elmer deposit his mother's check.

I watch Elmer sing through his telephone, ordering Reggie to come by after work.

I watch Elmer contemplate a job at Wash N' Fluff.

I watch Elmer think of Pinky's honey-like scent.

I watch Elmer exhaling perfect smoke rings.

I watch Elmer imagine Pinky, bottomless.

I watch Elmer picture himself steering limousines toward drunken proms.

I watch Elmer gently peck his wrist, pretending it's hers.

I watch Elmer defecate and wipe himself three times.

I watch Elmer say, aloud, "I can't wait any longer."

Reggie tells himself he'll vanish just like his mother. He longs for moments of joy, but he feels certain he'll pay for all his sins. His skull rocks with hopeless flurry.

Prayer.

Hospital beds.

Dr. Dann.

Injections.

Scowling nurses.
Pudding.
Prayer.
Disgrace.
Diseases.
Bedpans.
Prayer.
Loveless.
Prayer.
Prayer.

Elmer scales up the filthy steps, each clomp boomeranging through the crooked stairwell. Pinky's tiny koala bear sits inside his t-shirt pocket. He stops before her door, raps gingerly.

Apartment three groans open. Pinky, small and soft, leans before him in a nightgown. Fiery ringlets waterfall from her head, pouring beyond her shoulders. Her hands hide a drowsy smile.

"Hi, Pinky," Elmer says.

"Hi."

"How you doin'?" he asks. "You alright?"

"Yeah," she says, tee-heeing quietly.

Elmer pinches out the animal and kisses her cheek with its snout. "Here," he says, smiling. "Won this for you at the arcade."

Pinky cradles the bear like an emerald. "That's sweet, Elmer."

"I just wanted to do something ... so you'd know I was thinking about you. I guess it's dumb."

"It's not dumb. It's terrific."

I know that Elmer's entire body wrings when Pinky says 'terrific.'

She tells him, "I like *all* the animals you bring me. They fill up my entire bed." Pinky hides another smile.

He asks, "So ... what's this about your TV?" He begins to bumble behind the dusty, black and white television. Elmer untangles cords and stuffs in plugs.

Pinky asks, "Is it broken?"

"I can't really tell."

"Only one channel comes on. Seven."

"Maybe your TV finally shit the bed."

"Well, my mom gave it to me when I was fifteen," she says.

He grins. "Too old."

"Maybe. Yeah."

Elmer brushes off his freshly ironed flannel shirt. An old Christmas gift from Reggie he's never worn.

Pinky says, "At least I've got one channel, right?"

"You need *real* cable."

She sits on the edge of the ruffled bed. Elmer eases down beside her. Stuffed elephants, cats and button-eyed puppies surround them.

He says, "I can get you a new tube."

"You don't have to."

"I think my Mom has a spare."

"*Don't.* This one's fine," she says, smoothing her nightgown over her lap.

"You need something better. No biggie. I'll take care of it."

Pinky crisscrosses her shiny, powdered legs.

I have watched Elmer tend to this girl. Only part-time at first, but soon, non-stop: Frozen dinners, Shasta, stuffed reindeer, phone calls, pansies, Crackerjacks, Ambisol at three in the morning. Some days, on his most marvelous days, Elmer can coax Pinky out into the world for a brief stroll down Nixon Avenue.

"How about a walk tomorrow?" he asks.

"Well ... I dunno."

"You've got to get out, Pinky."

"I know, but I like it in here."

"Just say 'maybe.'"

"We'll see."

Elmer sighs.

Pinky says, "You must hate me. You must think I'm a freak."

"No. You're ... terrific. Like *you* always say."

A giraffe plummets to the floor. Carefully, Pinky scoops up the animal and returns it to the rest. "Do you have cologne on?" she asks.

"No. Just new deodorant."

"Smells nice."

"It's called 'Mountain Scent.'"

"Mountains don't smell, I don't think. Or do they?"

"Maybe they do. We should go and find out."

"Want to watch Jeopardy?" Pinky asks. "It's about to start, on my one channel. I have Cracker Jacks too."

For thirty-five minutes they sit, side by side, crunching on caramel nuggets and gazing at the snowy trivia show.

I know that there are no surprises in their boxes.

Reggie spots Maria's corn cart steaming on the sidewalk. He sees buttered cobs, silk, pails, root beer, salt shakers, napkins, salsa.

"Hey, Reggie," Maria calls out. She jiggles, clad in shorts and towering heels.

Stray whiffs of corn stalk the atmosphere, swabbing Reggie's face. "Hey, Maria," he replies.

She pumps and twirls beside her radio.

"You look great today!" he says.

"Thanks, honey. Wanna ear?"

"Can't. Have to get to work. I'm late."

Since always, I have watched Maria wheel around town, selling corn. She has sashayed down Pleasant Ave, Sixth Street, West Street, and year after year, she has become more like a lady.

She asks, "See my new top?" Maria pokes her nails at the frilled jersey that clings to her body. "Got it at the mall last week. Discount."

"Pretty."

"For real?"

"For real."

"So … ya still cleanin' up that church?" she asks.

"Yep."

"Don't you hate it, Reggie?"

"Someone's got to do it," he shrugs. "And I like it there. It's quiet. It's close to God."

"When I was a little *boy*, my mama used to make *me* go to church. Hated it. Bet they wouldn't let me in now."

Reggie dips his head to the right. "The lord accepts everyone."

"You're the *only* catholic who thinks so. Remember to say a prayer for me, honey."

He smiles, smiles, smiles. "I will. I always do."

"And keep your eyes open. I gotta find a new job. Need some money. Wanna finish my operation before next Christmas. Know of anything?"

"Don't think so."

"I *hate* my penis," she says, fake-glowering.

Elmer is watching suited men debate on television. He sees their brows are damp, their smiles faux. He thinks, *Come up with a solution! Cooperate, don't debate!* In sixth grade, Elmer Mott ran for class President. His mother was swiftly stirred, helping to make pins and posters. Even 'VOTE FOR ELMER' sweat bands. There were no debates, but Elmer did champion for a cola machine. The students raved about Coke, RC, Crush. But Elmer soon found his platform unfair since a young Mormon boy named Gregory wasn't allowed sugar. Elmer's campaign soon shriveled. Classmates drew genitals on his signs. He lost.

Elmer clicks off the coverage.

I know he longs for a truly fair and honest system. A system yet to be conjured.

Earlier, Reggie had slipped inside St. Leo's church and crept toward the giant statue of Jesus Christ. He had stared into his sad, dark, droopy eyes. "I'm sorry," he'd said, "You must hate me for all of this … for all these years." Even earlier, Reggie had dashed into Vic's Variety to buy one long snake of two-dollar scratch tickets. Fast Cash. Now, stretched along a polished pew, he scratches off each card, searching for a jackpot.

Red splinters of light slice into the silent church. Searing beams pour through visions of a stained-glass angel. The savior trumpets and he looms.

Reggie Lauderdale scratches off his final lotto box.

Nothing.

Reggie begins to pray, "Lord … please make my condition go away." He sweeps metallic lotto shavings into his palm, neat and prim. "I know I ask a lot from you, but please, please don't punish me. And don't hate me. 'Cause *I try*. I *could* be better, but I'm not *that* bad. And I like me. And I hope … I hope you like me too." As Reggie's prayers flutter from the balcony and bound through the chapel, he gives into a quiver. "Hear my prayer, O Lord; let my cry come to thee. Do not hide my face from thee in the day of my distress."

Patsy Cline croons from Elmer's childhood home.

He lollops down a path rimmed in pansies, creepers and marigolds. Samson, his half-blind, brown terrier, stumbles behind. Grubby, shabby, the dog collides with a boulder. He yelps and rises, but continues to follow Elmer.

His father crouches down, beneath a maple canopy. He rips out dainty, blonde buttercups from the earth. Once removed, he shakes away the soil from their roots. Mr. Mott groans, stretching to his six full feet. Like always, his face is askew. Red. Turned up. Slicked with lawn clippings. Seven seconds pass before he glances at his son.

Elmer asks, "What are you doing, dad?"

His father swabs his sweaty forehead. "I was gonna rip out all my flower beds, but the heat brought 'em back to life. We'll probably get a frost tonight. Be just my luck. Ahhh, fuck it. Might as well do it now."

"You don't have to get rid of them."
"Why not?
"They're still alive."
"Well, they're mine and I'll toss 'em if I want."
Elmer sighs. "Where's Mom?"
"The Wholesale Shop," he replies.
"Oh."
Mr. Mott stoops down and yanks out a cluster of impatiens. His glasses slip further down his nose. He says, "Your mother always stocks up on big jars of junk we don't need. Mayo. Salad dressing, steak sauce. Cocktail wieners too. I have those damn things for lunch every day."

Elmer peers around, then asks, "Hey, uh, what happened to the TV that used to be in the basement?"
"It's still in the basement."
"Could I use it? I need it."
"For what?
"For Pinky."
His father frowns, shakes his head. "That girl? In your building?
"Yeah."
"You getta job, yet?"
Elmer huffs quietly. "No. I've been lookin', though."
"Listen up. After your birthday, your mother and I ... we're not going to pay for your rent and food anymore. You have to grow up, Elmer. You're twenty-four years old. You finished college. And now, you have to make your own money."
"I know, dad. Alright."
Mr. Mott rubs the dirt from his hands. "Remember? I already said that you're welcome to drive cars with me."
"Yep."
"It'd be easy. I'll buy a new black stretch and business would double. Triple. And when I retire, it'll all be yours."

I know that Elmer sees his father as a sturdy, fixed, faceless skyscraper. Even when he was six, ten, twelve, this father never changed. Grumbles about work ... grumbles about money ... stillness ... stillness ... questions ... more grumbles ... and stillness again.

Samson pops out a bark.
"Shut it," Mr. Mott commands.
"I'll go get the TV," Elmer whispers.

Reggie troops down the aisle, sweeping up the remains of a wilted bouquet. He pushes petals into neat miniature piles and for a mini moment, pretends he's marching toward someone for himself.

Yes, yes. I have seen him parade like this before. And every time he's glazed with hope. A speck of sadness too.

Behind Reggie, the double doors split open.

"Hi, Father Fink" he calls out.

"Hello, Reg."

"I'll be finished soon. I'll be quick."

"It's fine. No need to rush." The man's hairless head gleams in the light.

"The ceremony was really ... *great*. I liked everything you said."

"Thanks."

"Your weddings are the best," Reggie says.

I know that Reggie can always be found at weddings and Sunday services. I have seen him, enraptured by the vows, the hymns, the speeches, the songs. And I hear Reggie's questions that always perform pestering back flips inside his mind. *Does God hate sinners before he forgives them? Can God hear me? Does God grant every prayer ... especially when you're good? Will I ever get married? Before God?* Reggie sweeps more and says, "What a mess, huh?"

"I hear you."

"Yeah."

"No, Reggie. *I hear you.*"

He triple-blinks. "What do you mean, Father Fink?"

"When you pray. Up there in the pews."

Reggie's face quickly jewels in sweat. "I'm sorry."

"Don't be," he says. "It's wonderful."

"Well, if I ever get too loud, just tell me. I'll stop."

Father Fink chuckles. "I'll be sure to let you know. Feel like confessing today?"

"Um, not today. Don't think I have enough yet."

"Saving up, eh? Well, we all wander and stray."

"I try not to," Reggie says.

"Me too. Hey, feel like going to this reception with me? Free spaghetti supper. Dancing, if you like that. Nice catholic girls all dressed in pink."

"Can't. Gotta finish up here."

"Okay."

"I'll bring shepherd's pie on Tuesday."

"Perfect. We'll eat while you confess."

On the pimpled sidewalk, Elmer is perched atop his parent's television set. He and Mrs. Lolly have been gabbing, gossiping and chatting since four. They munch on oyster crackers as the power lines sway above Nixon Avenue.

Mrs. Lolly asks, "So ... ya gonna be a fancy chauffer?"

"Don't wanna."

"But will ya?"

"Not sure. Maybe," Elmer says.

Mrs. Lolly wets her smile with candied gulps of blackberry brandy. Seemingly ablaze, she reaches out and pets his shabby hair. "Gotta make your own life, boy." "But I don't really know what I want to do," he says.

"So, ya ain't got no idea 'bout thangs?" she asks.

"Nope."

"Yo daddy's right, Elmer. It's time to grow up."

"Yeah, yeah."

"Well, what did ya learn at college?"

"Communications."

She grimaces, sips some more. "What's *that*? *Communications*?"

"It's nothing, really," he says, beginning to laugh. "I got a degree in nothing."

Elmer crunches a handful of small, salty discs. He thinks, *Since I can't be president or mayor or governor, I could be like Mrs. Lolly, sit in a chair and happily watch the world prance by*. She tells him, "I bet you'd like to just take care of Pinky for a livin'."

"Wouldn't be so bad," he says and chews.

"You already do an A plus job, Elmer."

Reggie mashes his face against the screen door. He hears another ballgame root and roar on the AM radio.

"Dad? Dad?"

There is no response. Reggie wonders if maybe he tumbled down the stairs, or swallowed the wrong pills. Maybe his heart stopped, like he always said it would.

"Dad?"

Nothing.

"Hey! Daaaaaad!"

The boy scrambles inside and eases down the cluttered hallway. He sees stacks of newspapers, coffee cans, empty wine bottles, jam jars, two snow shovels. Quickly, Reggie opens the bathroom door. An immediate stink swarms him.

His giant father shouts, "I'm taking a BM!" Mr. Lauderdale sits on the toilet, bumbling through last Sunday's crossword puzzle. Shirtless, his prickled rolls of skin bulge and ruffle along his three-hundred-pound frame. His bellybutton is the size of a half-dollar.

Reggie turns away and asks, "Didn't you hear me calling?"

"No, kiddo. Think I'm going deaf. Falling apart."

"Tell the doctor. And what about your foot?"

"Dr. Dann gave me more antibiotics. It's hooey, I think. That stuff don't work on me anymore. I have to take two or three pills every time."

Reggie asks, "You feel okay?"

"Yeah. Just gotta take it easy," his father says. White scars swerve over Mr. Lauderdale's back like kinked fencing. Reggie says, "No more walks to Vic's Variety, Dad."

"Not for a while."

Reggie scratches at his forearm. A tiny, red splotch shaped like Tennessee has spread across his skin. "I think I'm getting a rash," he says, almost whispering.

His father asks, "Can ya come over and do groceries next Friday?"

"Can't. I'm supposed to be some place."

"Where?"

"Church. There's a wedding," he replies.

"Well, after that?"

"Maybe before."

Mr. Lauderdale pushes out more mess. It plops into the bowl of water. He says, "Dr. Dann's secretary told me ya had some kinda problem with your ... *you know* ... ding dong."

Reggie hollers, "Dad! Don't ..."

"Well, is everything okay down there?"

"Yeah. It's just ... I just ... keep having those dreams. I can't make them stop."

His father sighs, smelling his index finger. "You been prayin'?"

"Of course." Reggie's eyes wheel backwards.

"You been confessin'?"

"Every week, dad."

"Mmm. Well, maybe try Bengay. That might work."

In spite of all the jeers, the Red Sox are still losing by only one point.

"I gotta wipe," his father says.

"Alright. I'll make some BLT's"

"Oh, hey, Dolly called."

"What'd she say?"

"She and Herb are off to their little paradise island. Must be the life, huh?"

"Yeah. Paradise."

Elmer re-reads his letter.

Mr. President
1600 Pennsylvania Avenue NW
Washington, DC 20500

Dear Sir,

Hello. It's Elmer Mott again.
You have only responded once to my letters, and, quite frankly, I am sure you did not write it yourself. Was it some intern? Or do you have a generic letter saved some place and when goons like me send you a note, you whip it out and stamp your name? It's fine. I take no offense. I know that you're busy with things.
The election is coming up and I bet you're nervous. I do hope you win! The other guy seems like a jerk, so, yeah, I hope you win.
I still think the process of election is way more complicated than it needs to be. It doesn't make sense. Electoral College votes are stupid. It makes the whole thing too drawn out. It should be like this: Two people make their speeches and their promises and then the country votes. Simple. And someone from somewhere else should count the votes. A guy in Canada! That way it's fair. And that way, the people of the United States of America truly choose their leader. This is only my opinion, of course.
Since the election is so near, I just want to urge you to NOT run childish, attacking commercials. For two reasons. First, that's not very nice and it makes you look like an asshole. Two, if I fall asleep on the couch with the TV on, those ads come on and they seem much louder than the others. So, they wake me up!
More from me later.

Sincerely,

Elmer Mott

Reggie slumps before the mirror and unscrews the tub of green jelly. He digs in four fingers, scoops out a massive gob, and smells the Bengay. Its minty aroma spanks his senses. Reggie swabs himself. Penis. Testicles. Anus.

He prays, "Oh my God, I am heartily sorry for having offended thee and I detest all my sins because I dread the loss of heaven and the pains of hell, but most of all because they offend thee, my God, who are all good and deserving of all my love. I firmly resolve, with the help of thy grace, to confess my sins, to do penance and to amend my life."

I also feel Reggie's flesh scorching.

After eighteen knocks, Elmer sighs and sets the television outside Pinky's door. He thinks of shouting her name, but simply sulks back to his apartment. He slams his door and the American flag on his wall flutters.

"Fuck," he says.

Elmer yanks off his pants. He slips his penis in between the couch cushions. He swerves and gyrates. He pinches his nipples, too.

I know that Elmer is daydreaming about her. I know he thinks that Pinky's mouth could cover him completely.

Reggie wipes his genitals clean.

When he was seven years old, he felt as though his mother could see him all the time, even with doors sealed tight. Even with blinds cranked shut. Reggie could say, *I feel sick*, and his mother would have replied *I know*. He could have said, *I stole quarters from your purse*, and she would have replied, *I know*. He could have said, *I'm feeling sinful*, and she would have replied, *Yes. And so am I.*

Right now, he hopes his mother will not watch.

Topless and potbellied, Elmer glugs on a beer. He is sprawled across the butterscotch sofa. He listens for Pinky, for the girl who hides above. The plunks of her remote control. The swill of a toilet. A cupboard closing. Elmer, though, finds nothing but bleak silence.

His door unlocks, the hinges keening.

Reggie shuffles through. He strips off his loafers and wiggles his toes. Reggie points to the brew. "How many you had?"

Elmer pats his belly. "Only, like, two," he says, and belches. "Maybe three. Is it a sin to be a drunk like me?"

Elmer always becomes amped when tossing jest and jabs at his cousin.

"Enough," Reggie says.

"Am I going to *burn*? Am I going to catch fire?" Elmer gut-chuckles. "Ha! I'm going to hell!" he shouts.

Reggie folds his arms. "No. *You'll* be fine. I pray for you because you won't pray for yourself."

"That's stupid."

"Why?"

"We're all going to die, like, seriously sleep. Cold in the ground."

Reggie sits by Elmer's feet. He says, "*You* can believe what *you* want to believe and *I* can believe what *I* want to believe."

Elmer stammers, "You're too good, Reg. You're too wound up. Like a nun. I mean ... don't you wanna be bad sometimes ... even just a little."

Reggie's face softens and quickly becomes blank. "*No.*"

Swigging back the last of his beer, Elmer burps. He toe-taps his cousin—laughs once more—springs up—locks an arm around Reggie—wrestles him to the rug.

"Let me go!" Reggie squeals, amid giggles.

"Not till you're bad. Not till you swear or say something."

"Stop!"

"Just say 'shit.'"

"No! *El*mer!"

"Say 'ass.' Say 'asshole.'"
"Get off me!"
"Swear," Elmer commands.

Gasping, tittering, wheezing, coughing, Reggie finally whispers, "Shit."

Elmer rouses with victory. "Ha! See! It's easy, right?"

"*Elmer* ..."

"I'm just having fun. Don't add this to your list. Okay? Don't. It's *my* fault."

Elmer says, "You haven't said anything about my sign out front."

"So ... you're running for president?"

"Yeah. I'd do better than the dickholes in charge. Bunch of liars."

Reggie asks, "Okay. What party have you joined?"

"Neither. They both blow. I'm starting my own party. *I'm* checking the box that says 'other' and I'm entering in my own name."

"What would *you* do as president?"

Elmer drums his paunch. "I'd feed the hungry. I'd kill AIDS. I'd build houses for bums. I'd make USA ... *awesome*."

"Then I'd vote for you." Reggie plops down on a vinyl hassock.

Elmer asks, "Are you registered?"

"Well, I don't know. I don't think so. No."

"*That's* a sin."

"Really?"

"Yes, Reg. You want these jerks running our country?" Elmer asks.

"I guess not. *No*. I'll register. Promise. For real."

Elmer scratches his armpits. "You better, cous."

"Do me a favor. Come with me to a wedding next Friday? I hate going alone."

"Who has a wedding on a Friday?"

"These people, I guess."

Elmer asks, "Who are *these* people?"

"Don't know them," Reggie says. "But I know that she's gonna have these glass angel things and a glittery carpet. I heard them talking with Father Fink."

"Yeah, okay. I'll go."

Reggie glances at the VCR's flaring, gleaming digital clock. "It's 10:10. Time to make a wish."

I have watched this ritual since they were small boys. Reggie is dazzled by double digits as if they're charmed. A chance for prospect. He has always begged Elmer to join in. I know that, despite his protests, Elmer enjoys it.

Reggie pleads, "Come *on*. We only have a minute. Please?"

"Fine."

I see both boys close their eyes. While the room becomes hushed, they cast out their wishes with clamped fists and earnest souls.

After some time, Elmer finally asks, "What did you wish for?"

"For Christ to forgive me," Reggie replies.

"He doesn't have to forgive you because you haven't done anything wrong. You always ask for the same thing."

"Well, I really want it to come true. What did *you* wish for?"

"For Pinky."

"Well, you always wish for the same thing too."

"Yeah, well …"

"Did you walk with her today?"

Elmer's shoulders hike up, then flop back down. "Nope."

I feel Elmer bury his fuss, his worry, his defeat.

Reggie whispers, "There's something wrong with her. I mean, no one is perfect, but …"

"She's just scared."

"She's … sick."

Elmer flicks his hand. "She's agoraphobic. I looked it up. I think she's getting better, though."

"Maybe she'll come out tomorrow," Reggie says.

"Maybe," Elmer replies, guzzling a fresh can of beer.

"Can we watch my show?"

"I wanted to watch the debates again. Funny. *I* didn't get an invitation."

"Please?"

"*Fine.*" Elmer nabs the remote and punches *ON*. News of five more heat-soaked days dart across the screen. Elmer says, "Global warming. Also a sin." He clicks through sitcoms, reruns, a breast cancer commercial, straight to channel fifty-eight.

The boys watch a dark, round man howl at a pack of elders, screaming threats of damnation, loneliness. Reverend Rockwell thrusts his hands into space. He cries, "The Lord will absolve you! The lord will embrace you. He looks beyond cruelty, spite, malice, sloth. HE knows that we are faulty. We fall. We fail. We create ruin. We make a thousand mistakes every single day … and it's okay … because the Lord will welcome YOU!"

Reverand Rockwell conjures hollers and loud 'amen's'.

I see them listen.

I see them watch.

CHAPTER TWO
ANGEL BOY

Reggie is folded on the chapel steps. Afternoon bells ring loud. Bing, bong. Bing, bong. He unwraps his stuffed, mangled jelly sandwich. Preserves gush, drooling from each side.

A taxi cab veers to the curb, mere feet away. A boy, eyes bright as glitter balls, climbs from the car. Reggie hears him say, "Oops. Wish I had some change for ya, fella." His words are soaked in a southern twang. "*Real* sorry," he says.

The driver shakes his head, throttles away.

Reggie begins to devour his lunch. He bites and chomps and swallows and sips. He pretends to be invisible.

"Hey," the boy says.

Reggie peers up.

Trousers hang on his hips. "You in the choir too?"

"Oh. No. I just work here."

Pimples pock the boy's forehead and cheeks. "When does practice start?"

"They usually meet at four-thirty."

"My grandma said *four*," he grouses. "I'm fuckin' *early*."

Reggie sighs and shakes his head with annoyance.

"Oh. *Yeah*. Pardon," he says in a sleepy drawl. "This *is* a church. I ain't supposed to talk that way."

Reggie can smell sour whiffs that sweep out from the boy's underarms. "So, you in the new group?" he asks.

"Yeah," he says, "Since we moved, Grandma's been gettin' at me to join. Heard me singin' in my room one night. Now she won't let up 'bout it."

"You must be good."

"*Naw. I* don't think so. But grandma tells the whole neighborhood I sing like an angel."

Reggie's eyes flicker. "Where are you from?"

"Alabama." The stranger sits beside him. He squints at Reggie, smirks and cackles loudly.

"Why are you laughing?"

"Ya got jelly on ya."

Reggie napkins his mouth.

The boy glances around the barren street, bunches the sleeve of his sweatshirt and swipes Reggie's lips. "Ya didn't get it all."

"Thanks."

"No big deal. This gotta go in the wash soon anyhow."

"Oh."

I know Reggie cannot ignore the buzz that spills from deep inside. The boy asks, "Hey, think I could have a bite of your sandwich?"

Reggie ponders bacteria, disease. "I don't know you."

"It's not like I got AIDS."

Reggie then ponders AIDS, herpes, abscesses.

"My stomach's doin' back flips, is all. Haven't eaten since supper."

Reggie clicks off his reeling mind. "Okay. Here. Have the rest."

"All I need's a bite." He takes the battered sandwich and smiles. The stranger says, "Lemme see if I can remember this one right… Bless us Lord, and these gifts, which we are about to receive, from the bounty… through Christ, our Lord. Amen."

"Yep. You got it." Reggie grins.

The boy snaps off a hunk. Quickly, he passes it back to Reggie. "Your turn," he says.

Visions of death-inducing germs return.

"Don't worry. I'm clean," the boy says. "I'm all good."

"It's okay." Reggie lies. "I'm full."

The boy sucks the jam off his fingers, "I'm Vern."

Reggie thinks of his father's sixty-year old friend, Vernon, and another elderly church go-er called Vern. Reggie says, "You have an old man's name." He laughs.

"Well…I'm only fuckin' nineteen. Ain't *that* old."

Reggie huffs once more. Pestered.

"Sorry," Vern says. He reaches over and wrenches the hair on Reggie's arm. "Sorry 'bout my foul mouth. Again."

"It's fine."

"Fine."

Reggie dumps his hand inside his sack. "Want some potato sticks?"

Elmer lies on his bed, half-hard.

He has memorized Pinky's elbows, each one set with three curved nuggets of bone. The largest sits in the center, covered in creamy whiteness. Two smaller nubs embrace the midpoint. Sometimes they jut. Sometimes they sink. Depends on what she's doing.

I know that Elmer has always wanted to grasp Pinky's elbow and steer her along as they stroll to a flea market or a roller rink, or a thrift store, or a go-cart racetrack. But Pinky always shrinks away.

Right now, Elmer is held captive by the charm of a lighters flame. He watches the tiny blaze skitter, lean and jump. Glazed in boredom, he carefully presses the fire to his calf. A strip of hair singes, burning to shriveled black corkscrews.

The telephone rings.

"Hello?"

"I'm ready to go," Pinky says

"Really? You sure?"

"Yeah."

"I'll be up in two secs."

"Terrific."

Elmer lifts five fingers to the sun. "Look, it's beautiful. Almost feels like summer again. I love this stuff. Eighty in November. Sort of feels fake, though."

Pinky pulls at her nightgown. She has slipped into bright, pristine sneakers.

Elmer trots ahead and swiftly stops, walks backwards, facing Pinky. "Hey …"

"Yes?"

"You look pretty today."

She bops her head to the left. "Sure."

"You do. You *always* do, though."

Their steps cut through the middle of Nixon Avenue. Pinky and Elmer stroll past beat-up, faded double-decker homes. He stomps on each manhole cover and laughs, hoping to catch a smile from Pinky's fretting face.

Elmer asks, "Don't you ever miss this? The outside?"

I see that Pinky is startled. She backs away from children grinding about on Big Wheel bikes.

He says, "I mean…you don't see much of anything else … so you must miss it."

Pinky hugs herself. "No. Not really."

"Why?"

"Because it's just … it's safer inside."

"How's that?"

"I'm pathetic. I know," she tells him. "I'm a basket case." Pinky sighs. "It's just … in my room, I don't feel nervous and I don't feel afraid."

He lights a cigarette as they round a corner.

"I know I seem nuts, Elmer."

"Do you *feel* nuts?"

Pinky hesitates, "Some days."

"Can't you go and, like, get help?" he asks. Elmer stumbles and almost falls to the stained street.

"I did when I was a kid. I saw this doctor. And he still sends pills to my mom in Torrance and she sends them on to me. It helps. I think."

"That's good. That's *really good*."

"Sometimes, though, I feel like I wanna chop my head off so I don't have to think anymore. I hate how I think. I hate my brain."

With a rascal grin, he replies, "Don't chop your head off. I like your head." She giggles. "Hopefully, someday, I'll wake up and everything will change. I'll feel terrific all the time. So terrific I can go to Las Vegas and Atlantic City. I don't know."

Elmer has a deep urge to say, *I'll take you there. And you won't be frightened. You won't worry about a thing.* But he does not speak.

"Think we could head back in a minute?" Pinky asks.

"Whatever you want."

Reggie stares at the Virgin Mary, but thinks of Vern. His tart smell. His shoulders, his filthy fingernails. His voice. His specific sort of swagger.

Reggie polishes Mary, buffing her body clean. His wad of paper towels is streaked with dust and grime. Reggie begins to scrub her breast, stops, but continues on.

"Reggie?"

He turns to see Father Fink. "Oh. Good morning."

Father Fink says, "Maybe don't do that. Mary's old. And I'm not sure she likes being … washed there."

"Sorry. But she's real dirty. Like she hasn't been washed in a million years."

"Well, we want to keep her the way she's always been."

"I just want to do a good job," Reggie says.

"Oh, *yes*. No problemo. So … how's it going?"

"I'm okay," he replies.

"I heard you praying for forgiveness earlier."

"I do. Every day."

Father Fink wipes his forehead and says, "Just be patient."

"Waiting is hard." Reggie leans on the saint and rubs her cloaked head.

"I know," Father Fink replies.

He thinks of his bulky, blimp-sized sin. He thinks of his

punishment, his possible disease. Reggie asks, "How *long* do I have to wait?"

"Lord, no one knows."

"Do you think…if you're a good person … if you really try, that God will forgive you and make all your, you know, wishes come true?"

"I'd have to say yes. I think so. I'd bet that's true."

Reggie is squinting. "I thought you'd know for sure."

It ticks closer to 5 A.M. Drowsy, Elmer watches the political debate once more. He sees men smile, wag fingers, pose, shake hands, grin, raise fists. These men continue to dodge everything that has crunched up America. Petting his penis, Elmer proclaims, "Jerks! *I* should be the fucking president."

Reggie's tonsils are poked. He clutches a fat cloud while Christ crams himself inside the boy's mouth. Reggie is choking on the savior's scent. Earth, muck, sweat.

Jesus shouts, "Come o holy spirit, fill the hearts of your faithful and enkindle in them the fire of your love."

"Jesus," Reggie moans.

The savior jerks free. Rollicking, he flips Reggie over and pries apart his rear. He hollers, "Send forth your spirit and they shall be created! And you shall renew the face of the earth!"

Jesus enters and instantly Reggie feels ablaze, as if bonfires rumble at his core.

Then, he awakes.

Rousing and sad. Damp, befuddled. Hot, crazed.

Reggie strips and begins to tidy himself with a tube sock. Absently, he pinches a puny lump on his right testicle. Swells of ache pulse through him.

"Oh, God.," he whispers.

It's Election Day and Elmer is impatient. A red taxi-cab has idled in front of ninety-nine Nixon Avenue for ten minutes. Elmer has been pacing, smoking, apologizing to the driver.

Finally, Mrs. Lolly inches from her first-floor apartment, donning a new wig and neon pink lips.

"Meter's running...*still*," Elmer announces.

"When you take a dame out on a date yo' not supposed to talk 'bout cab fare 'fore she gets out the goddamn door."

"*You* asked *me* out," Elmer says, his eyes eclipsed by massive shades.

"Well, I hope ya plan on romancin' me, baby."

Elmer juts out his left arm like a wing. Mrs. Lolly latches on. Together, they scramble inside the cab.

Elmer says, "City Hall, sir."

As they motor off, buildings blur by.

Mrs. Lolly asks "Why'd ya have to pick now to go an' vote? Ya cut my snooze in half."

"It's two. No lines."

Mrs. Lolly scoops through her purse and digs out a can of Moxie cola. She pops it open and indulges with loud, slurping gulps. "Did ya check yo mail today?"

"I check my mail, like, once a month," he says.

"Check it, then, 'cause the landlady sent us all a letter sayin' she's gonna get ridda the lead paint and we gotta be out by next Saturday. Eight in the mornin'!"

Elmer is jarred by an immediate smack of angst. "What the fuck?"

"Yes. *What the fuck.* And we can't come back until Monday morning," Mrs. Lolly says, slurping again.

"What about Pinky?"

"Don't she check her mail neither?"

"She hates the lobby. It makes her nervous."

"Christ."

Elmer tries to crank the window down, but it locks half-way. "What's she gonna do?"

Elmer stands inside a wooden booth. He has not swept the red, white and blue curtain closed. With a silent beer burp, he blacks out both presidential candidates. Carefully, he prints his name.

Chunky capital letters. ELMER MOTT.

Soaring through side streets, the meter reads, "$14.14."

Elmer rubs patterns into the grain of his corduroy slacks. Light, dark. Light, dark.

Mrs. Lolly says, "Thanks for takin' me, baby."

"Who'd you vote for?"

She grins. "Elmer Mott."

"Good girl."

Reggie waits in examination room four. He is usually ushered to room two or three. Not today. Reggie recalls his mother's final hours. With crumpled paper skin, she'd said, "I always wanted to be a blonde bombshell, Reggie. Like you. Like Marilyn. And I wanted to be taller too. Tall people really grab folks' attention. But heels are for sinners, sweetie." Her lips were caked with orange Jello rot. Her body had puffed from medication, chemotherapy.

Reggie prays they reunite in heaven. His father had once said she might be in hell. He'd said, "I think she was envious. She had idols. She worshipped stars. She wanted to be in pictures, you know." Reggie is certain she has been embraced by the Lord. One day, he too, will hold her again.

Reggie is like his mother. He, too, knows he must pay. He, too, knows there will be ultimate pain. He, too, fears the agony. Mustached nurses.

Clipboards.
Glassy corridors.
Catheters.
Small paper cups.
Frigid floors.
Vomiting.
Trips to the humid gift shop.
Injections.
Deflated balloons.
Prayer.

Dr. Dann clomps into the examination room, tipping back a large Styrofoam cup. He balks, he winces, he pounds his chest. "Have you tried the coffee at Vic's Variety?"

"No," Reggie says.

"*Don't.* It's mud."

"Vic can be ... forgetful."

"Nasty."

Reggie dangles his head.

"So ... what is it now, Reg?" Dr. Dann asks.

Reggie peers up. "I think ... I have a bump ... *down there.*"

"Where, specifically, *down there?*" he asks, sighing.

"My ... my testicle."

Dr. Dann folds his arms. "Reggie ... I'm going to tell you something and I don't want you to become, *you know,* upset."

"Okay."

"You're *not* sick. You *never* have been sick. You've *never* had an earache or the flu or conjunctivitis. But ... you're so afraid that something's wrong ... so afraid you're sick ... that you're missing out on life."

Reggie stops breathing and for a long, muddled minute, stares into Dr. Dann's pink eyes.

"You need to stop this," the doctor says.

"I'm sick," he replies.

"No. You're not."
"I can feel it. It's there."
"No."
"Yes."
"I don't want you to come back here, Reggie. Never again. And no more Emergency Room visits. No more ambulances. Or I'll tell your dad. Okay?"

⁂

I know that Elmer has thought of phoning the landlady to beg for more time.

I know that Elmer has thought of wrapping Pinky in electric blankets.

I know that Elmer has called The Red Roof Inn.

I know that Elmer has considered a plane, bound for Reno.

I know that Elmer has thought of his parent's moth-balled basement.

I know that Elmer has thought of Reggie's too-small apartment.

I know that Elmer has called his friend, Phil, from junior college.

I know that Elmer has considered legal action.

I know that Elmer has thought of pounding on Pinky's door, again.

I know that Elmer has thought of swigging another six-pack of brew.

⁂

The pews groan beneath Reggie. He tells Father Fink, "I hope you like the shepherd's pie." Reggie can barely spoon clumps of corn and beef into his mouth. He twitches, charged with fear.

Father Fink feasts, saying, "What a simply wicked dish, son."

"Thanks very much."

"You should spend some time in our soup kitchen."

Reggie hands over his list of sins.

"Oh. Yes. Of course. Confession time."

"You might be … upset."

"Don't be silly. Let's see. Curses. Littering. Yes …"

Reggie prays with gusto and might.

Father Fink grimaces. "Having impure thoughts about the Lord? What's *that* about?"

"Well … see. I'm sorry. I am. But these dreams. With Jesus. When we're doing … like …"

"Having intercourse?"

Tears swell in Reggie's brown eyes, swiftly overflowing and trotting down his cheeks. "I'm so sorry. I feel terrible. I've wanted to tell you."

"So, uh, has this been going on for long?" he asks.

"Yes," Reggie replies.

"Let me ask you a tricky question."

"Okay," he says, almost sniffling.

"Do you … do you like other fellas?"

"Well …"

"Do you?"

He whispers, "I think I do."

Father Fink asks, "You think? Or you *know*?"

"I think I know."

"Tell me about this."

Reggie pulls in a huge cloud of oxygen. "Well … I know … for sure that I can't help it and I can't change it and I don't think I *want* to. I've tried everything. I have."

"Go on."

Reggie says, "Well, I think it's pretty simple. I like what I like. I like fried clams, but I don't like onions. I could never eat one. I just don't like them. So … that's how I think about other boys." He coughs. "I like what I like and I think God made me … *like what I like*. Fried clams. Other boys. What do you think? Am I right?"

"The Lord made you and he made fried clams."

"Am I right?"

"I can't answer that, Reggie."

"Right. I got ya. So … do you think … do you think … God hates me?"

"Lord, no."

"Then I might just be okay after all?"

"I think you're going to be fine. And look, hey. Guess what? I like fried clams too."

Reggie sits on a sidewalk bench. He watches pink, hippo-sized clouds curtsy below the skyline. Joy boomerangs inside him. He feels somewhat free. He asks himself, *What if there is no punishment? What if all my dreams really will come true?* Reggie nips his testicle and the ache that follows reminds him of doom. Reggie, like always, begins to beg for mercy.

Vern shouts, "Hey! What are ya doin'?"

He tramps down the boulevard in blackened sneakers. He waves, he cocks his head, he chuckles, he hikes up his trousers, he spits, he chuckles again.

"Hi," Reggie says. A gigantic smile curves across his face, almost slicing his head in half. "I'm waiting for my ride," he says, "They always take a while."

"That stinks."

"How do you like the choir so far?"

Vern collapses beside Reggie. "Ah ... well, choir ain't the greatest thang in the world, but I like it when I get to sing. Lots of words to remember, though. And they're all about Jesus. But, hey, what did I expect, right?"

"Yeah."

"They ain't goin' to have us singin' 'bout sin." He laughs.

Reggie's forehead wrinkles. "I brought you something." He hands Vern a plastic container.

"What's this?" he asks, "a new life?"

"*No.* Shepherd's pie. Sometimes I bring lunch for Father Fink. I knew you'd be coming to practice, so ..."

Like a cap gun, Vern pops with laughter. "Wow," he says, "That's nice. That's *real* nice. What? You a do-gooder or somethin'?"

"No."

"You some kinda angel boy?"
Reggie reddens. "No."
"Well, this is ... just right."
A City Cab pulls up, tailing exhaust. The driver honks.
"Time to go." Reggie rises.
"Hey," Vern says, grabbing his wrist, "Thanks a lot."
"You're welcome, Vern. Are you singing at Friday's wedding?"
"I'm in the choir so ... I guess."
"Then I'll see you there."
"Okay. I'll try to catch ya." As the car chugs away, Reggie forbids himself from glancing back.

Elmer's father knots his bowtie. "Got a bunch of runs today," he announces.

Samson ticks around the living room. His mangy fur swishes. He collides with an end table, struggles back up and continues on. Elmer bends down to tug his ears.

"Did you vote?" Elmer asks his father.

"Busy day. I'll do it on the way home. Have to go to the vet too." His father begins moving boxes around.

"Does Samson need shots or something?"

"He's old. He's dirty. He can't see shit. He's always in the way."

Elmer frowns. "You're going to put him to sleep?"

"Yes. It's time. Don't be a cry baby, Elmer. So, anyway, your mother wanted to know about Thanksgiving. You comin' by for a free meal?"

Elmer yanks on his hair. "Sure. Yeah. Um ... I was thinkin' ... well ... my apartment's being painted or unpainted or whatever. And I was wondering ... Pinky and me don't have any place to go and Reggie's place is way too small ..."

"This isn't a motel," Mr. Mott says. "But there's plenty of 'em in town."

"You know I can't afford it, dad." "Then get a friggin' job. Be a man."

His father picks up Samson and places him inside a cardboard box labeled, *XMAS LIGHTS + ANGEL*.

I watch as Elmer's entire body clenches. He feels as though he's twelve again, squashed by the poundage of paper routes and the annual Boy Scout can drive. I know his father has always championed for a life he loathes. Now, Elmer's tight, knotted cords of anguish unfurl.

His father asks, "What are you going to *do*? What are you going to *be*? Are you going to end up a *bum*?"

"I'm not a bum, dad! I'm me."

"I don't want you to be a screw up!"

Elmer kicks the coffee table.

"Hey!" his father yells. "Watch it!"

"Can I ask you something?" Elmer says.

"What?"

"Am I a piece of shit? Is your only son a piece of shit?"

Mr. Mott laughs. "Stop acting like a sissy."

Elmer sweeps up Samson and hastily stomps off.

Elmer has trudged to the fields. Swallowed by tall reeds of grass, he opens the box and carefully lifts Samson out. Elmer playfully pulls on his poofy, knotted tail and gently places him on the ground. "I'd keep you if I could, Samson."

The dog stares up at Elmer with milky eyes. Samson scratches the dirt.

He leaps away.

Midnight looms and Reggie is binded in quilts.

Onscreen, Marilyn Monroe croons inside a studio half-shell. She is agleam and lustrous. She smiles while gems of light twirl around her.

Reggie quietly sings along, "I wanna be loved by you alone…"

He thinks of his mother. He remembers how she spoke of becoming this woman, how she hoped to become a glitzy icon. To Reggie, she was. Her penciled mole and hidden gowns. Her hats. Her strut. Her faux diamonds. Her sultry smiles and pear-shaped poses.

Reggie ponders Vern.

Reggie ponders his testicle.

He prays, "Lord, please make sure I'm not sick. And I hope I'm right. I hope I'm not an abomination." Reggie kneels. "Bless the Lord, oh my soul, and forget not all his benefits, who forgives all your iniquity, who heals all your diseases, who redeems your life from the Pit, who crowns you with steadfast love…"

Elmer watches the election results. His jack-in-the-box hand clicks and his middle finger salutes the screen. "Assholes," he says.

The new president raises both arms to a crowd that touts glossy banners of hope. Folks with glistened cheeks cheer in slackened ties. The winner waves, sporting a fashioned grin.

Elmer picks up the telephone. He dials Pinky, again. It rings. Rings, rings, rings, rings, rings, rings. Elmer called her during each commercial break and knocked on her door after lunch. He pounded again before the five o'clock news and after dinner, but still, she is silent.

I know that Elmer is stuffed with anguish.

I know that he is writhing with stress, non-stop.

Reggie went to the market and loaded a carriage with groceries for his father: chocolate chip cookies, chicken pot pies, three-cheese lasagna, spiced curly fries. Reggie bought fruit, too.

Now, tardy for Dr. Dann, Reggie bustles through the kitchen, stuffing food inside the already packed cabinets.

His father is sitting in the leaning recliner. His crimped bulges of skin are glossed in sweat. He pets his saucer-sized nipples. "Did you get ice cream bars?" Mr. Lauderdale asks.

"No, dad."

"But I asked you to. Twice." His father balks.

"Dr. Dann says you need to lose weight. So I got you good food, too."

"Did you get some turkey and biscuits for the holiday, at least?"

"No. But I will, dad. Of course," he says, hurriedly.

Mr. Lauderdale reclines even more, asking, "Remember when I used to be skinny?"

Reggie stops. "Things could be that way again."

"Nah."

Reggie sighs and steps into the living room. "You can do it, if you want to."

"But I don't want to. I just don't, Reg. Sweets make me happy. They're the only thing that makes me happy."

"What about God?" he asks. "He makes you happy."

"He doesn't come close, not anymore. Not at all. Awful. Isn't it?" Reggie's father picks up the remote control and mashes his beefy fingers into the buttons. Nothing happens. He whaps it thrice. "Damn batteries," he says.

"Dad … God makes you happy. He *does*."

"No. Not anymore. He took mom away. Sure, she was a sinner, but I loved her more than anything. The day she died, God ruined me. And I'm left to suffer. So now I'm a sinner too. I'm gluttonous. You think that's horrible? You think that's terrible?"

I watch Reggie walk over to the television and turn it on. Increasing the volume, he whispers, "Yes. It is terrible."

Mr. New President
1600 Pennsylvania Avenue NW
Washington, DC 20500

Dear Sir,

Hello.

I'd very much like to introduce myself. My name is Elmer Mott. I am twenty-four years old and sort of a politician like yourself.

Congratulations on becoming our new man in charge. You are not my first choice, but I guess one has to work with what they are given. Anyhow, I have a nugget of advice for you and it's this: Being the President of the United States of America is a pretty big job. You're the leader of the free world! No pressure, man!!! I'm not a dunce, so I know that there are many, many other people and corporations that help to make your decisions. Try to think about what the American people want, instead of making the assholes bigger assholes. Try making the American people better and finally happy. That's supposed to be your job, right? With fair, true order, comes harmony.

I hope this thought helps you along the way.

Please ... I ask you to prove me wrong. Don't be a corrupt liar, be a hero. So, congrats on your win and expect to hear from me soon.

Sincerely,

Elmer Mott

In Dr. Dann's waiting room, Reggie squirms in his chair. A senior sits beside him. The man cradles an oxygen tank as well as an issue of The Atlantic Monthly. He tips his porkpie hat saying, "This shit is boring." The man tosses the magazine, sucks from his plastic mask. "They never change the readers here."

"I know," Reggie replies.

"I want something goddamn ... *thrilling* to look at. A lady with real curves. A lady who could blow up the earth with just one wink of her eye. Look at me! I'm dying for fuck's sake."

"Yeah. Um ..."

"Pass me that one. The one with pretty gals on the front."

Reggie hands him a copy of the Enquirer. He notices that Jo Jo has returned to her desk. She looks at Reggie, glances away and squiggles on a form.

He races over and knocks on the faux glass.

"Why don't ya tell them to hurry it up?!" the old man shouts.

"Jo Jo, open up. Please?"

With lolling eyes, she whisks open the partition. "What do you need, Reggie?"

"Dr. Dann *has* to see me. I'm serious. There's a problem."

"He said you weren't a patient here anymore." She drinks from a can of ginger ale. "He said to tell you to go home."

"Why?"

"Look ... I'm sorry Reggie. That's what he told me. Okay?"

"This isn't fair."

She speaks quietly. "He's my boss, and ... I have to do what he says."

"He thinks I'm crazy. Doesn't he?"

"Yes."

The old man screams, "HURRY THE FUCK UP!"

Reggie asks, "But you don't think I'm crazy. Do you?"

"COME ON!"

"*Do you?*"

She shuts the Plexi-glass window.

CHAPTER THREE
TERRIFIC

Twenty-three minutes ago, Elmer propped stools in the yard. Earlier, he'd shoveled a ditch and plugged it with junk mail, receipts and soup cans. Seconds ago, Elmer sat beside Mrs. Lolly and tossed a match as they watched the blaze feed on garbage.

It's six-thirty now, and Elmer is smoking. Mrs. Lolly sips blackberry brandy.

He says, "Pinky won't answer me." He unspools a clump of toilet paper, pitching it to the flames. "What'll she do when we have to leave?"

"Well, Pinky ain't got *no* choice. She's gotta get out. We all do. And I'll tell her so."

"Don't talk so loud. She might hear you. What if her window's open?"

Mrs. Lolly clucks her tongue, exclaiming, "I could give two shits. Pinky gots to listen!"

Elmer slugs on a Meister Brau. "She *can't* leave. *Can't*. And there's nowhere to go."

"Like I said, she *gots* to."

"Well, then … whose adopting *you* for the weekend?"

"My sister. My sister who don't allow no drink in her home."

"Ooooh. Fuuuuuuun." Elmer cackles.

"Shut it, boy. That's why I be fillin' up while I can."

He sighs and smacks his knees.

Mrs. Lolly says, "Elmer … Pinky's grown. Ya got yo'self to worry 'bout."

An ambulance wails, braying through the streets.

Elmer sees Reggie appear. His curls look tousled. He wears a white T-shirt.

Mrs. Lolly waves and shouts, "Hi, baby!"

"Evening," Reggie replies. "Elmer? Why did you start a fire?"

"For dumb kicks," he tells him.

"The fire department's going to show up."

Elmer says, "Just sit. Relax. Calm down. This is the closest you'll get to hell. Enjoy it."

Reggie falls into a chair. He twitches.

Elmer asks, "What's the matter with you, anyhow?"

"Nothing."

Mrs. Lolly says, "Just tell us, child."

"I don't want to talk right now."

She pets his back. "Boy … let it out. Whateva's wrong."

"Well …"

"Go on," she urges.

"I think I'm sick," he says, his voice creaking. "I think I'm dying. I can feel it."

Mrs. Lolly laughs like gunfire. "Baby, I'm dyin' too. I've been dyin' since the day I was born. We all got somethin.' Ha!"

Elmer says, "You're not sick, Reg. You're just paranoid. You've always been paranoid."

Reggie leans on his fist. Knuckles cram his flesh.

Soon, these three slip into a pocket of silence.

I, too, watch as fire blackens the Boo Berry ghost, the grocery bags, and the election headlines.

Elmer topples onto the couch beside his cousin. He presses the remote control and Reverend Rockwell's *Night Praise* gleams to life. The man hollers, "Life is now! Life is today! You musn't waste the gift OUR Lord has given YOU." Elmer says, "I'm screwed, Reg."

"Because you lost the election?" He smiles and kicks off his loafers.

"Well, it *was* close. But, *no*. Really. I got problems. They want everyone out of here by Saturday. De-leading or some shit. What about Pinky?"

"Uh oh."

"Yep."

Elmer is wordless, jokeless, quipless. Two minutes stretch by.

Reverend Rockwell continues, "The power is in you! You can make all your dreams come to fruition! He has given you strength!" "Elmer?"

"Yeah?"

"I have to say something."

"Make it quick."

"I think I'm, like, I'm in love. *Maybe*."

Elmer's eyes fatten and his mouth turns slack. "With who?" he asks, "Maria?"

"Stop." "With *who*?"

Reggie almost gasps and says, "His name is Vern."

Elmer rises, charging toward his cousin. His grin is jumbo. He pinches Reggie's nose. He ropes his arms around him. Elmer squeezes, hard. "Congrats, Reg. This is … the *greatest*. You've … you've finally got it. I'm happy … I really am." Pride zooms through each inch of Elmer Mott.

The preacher on television yelps, "A NEW DAY IS NOW! A new beginning is any time YOU say. This is the start … of the start! Praise GOD!"

I watch Elmer release Reggie.

Reggie's smile flexes from small to large, again and again.

"This is awesome," Elmer says.

Reggie exclaims, "Hey! It's 11:11. Let's make our wish."

"Okay."

They shut their eyes.

I listen to the hopes of Elmer Mott and Reggie Lauderdale.

I feel sorrow for what has to follow.

Morning debuts.

Elmer's gavel-like fist beats on Pinky's door. He yells, "Shit, come on. We have to talk!"

Finally, her seven deadbolts unclick and release.

"Pinky …"

Her flesh is pale and creased from slumber. "Hi," she says.

The smell of seared popcorn stuffs her blacked out studio. Pinky is gripping a pair of scissors.

"What's … *up*?" Elmer asks.

"I thought you might be a burglar. I've been staying up late and watching the news and, well, people are murdered all the time."

"Why haven't you answered the phone? Or the door?"

She tugs on her nightgown. "I've been sleepy."

"You don't look so good."

"Sorry."

"I know that you know we gotta be outta here by Saturday."

Pinky sags her head, but swiftly snaps it up, forcing out a counterfeit smile. "Yeah. What a headache."

Elmer shrugs. "I'm worried about you. Where will you go?"

"Um, I called my mom and she's going to come get me. She's going to bring me to my aunt's. About five hours from here."

"How will you do that?"

"The doctor is sending some sort of pills. Mom says they'll knock me out for the ride." She coughs into her barreled hand. "Mom says I'll be fine."

"Okay," Elmer whispers. He chews on the inside of his cheek. Pinky says, "After all this, we'll go for a long walk. I promise."

"Sure." He turns and slowly descends the stairwell.

"Elmer?"

"Yep?"

"Thank you. I never tell you enough. So … *thank you*. You're a terrific guy."

Cameo's song, "Candy," boasts its beat.

Reggie has tied a striped Windsor knot around Elmer's neck and buffed two pairs of shoes. Today is a wedding day.

Reggie pleads, "Come on, Elmer. We can't be late."

St. Leo's Church hustles with attendees.

Reggie's eyes drink each detail. The streamers that sprawl, teeming like ballerina ghosts. The flowers that look like they've sprouted from pews and panels of wall. The suited men who laugh, shake hands, and smile at no one at all. Reggie shooshes Elmer, leading him up to a vacant balcony.

Elmer says, "Let me finish this joke."

"*Quiet.*"

"But it's a *real* knee slapper. Mrs. Lolly told me."

"Don't be a goof. We're in the Lord's house. God, Elmer."

I see both boys sit before the ledge.

Reggie says, "Behave."

"I'll try." Elmer snaps on Bazooka gum.

"Everyone looks so ... *happy.*"

"Or drunk."

"Ssshhh. Everything's perfect."

"Nothing's ever perfect, Reg."

"Well look at them," Reggie says, pointing. "I bet they *feel* perfect. It's like a postcard or an old photograph."

Elmer snickers. "You really love this crud, don't you?"

Reggie blushes, whispering, "I do."

Below them, a clan of choir folk begin to sing about splendor. About God. About love. Their honeyed voices embrace Reggie. He soon spots Vern. Vern has washed and combed his hair and on this night, a crisp, clean parted line rips down the left side of his head. He is covered in a gauzy robe.

Reggie is alight. "He's here."

"Which one?" Elmer asks, gnawing.

"The tall guy. With the blondish hair." "Hmmm. He looks alright." Elmer huffs out a huge bubble which promptly combusts, leaving behind a purple, chewing gum moustache. "He looks nice."

"He *is* nice."

Reggie watches while Vern croons with the others. Veins in his throat swell and stretch and dance and vanish. Reggie watches only this boy. Until the ceremony is complete.

Wedding goers shuffle out to the brightened street. Reggie and Elmer elbow against the flow of this one-way human traffic. When they reach the lectern, Vern squats down. He smiles as the other singers disperse.

"Well, hello," Vern says.

Reggie brushes a curl from his forehead. "Hi. This is my cousin. Elmer."

"I'm Vern."

"Yeah, and hey, great job up here. Reg's told me all about you."

"Good thangs or bad thangs?" he asks with a bandit grin.

Elmer has disappeared to suck on a cigarette.

Now, Reggie and Vern sit by the pulpit, legs bent like pretzels.

Vern says, "This outfit makes me look like a preacher's boy. Don't ya think? Like I'm pure and all?"

"It suits you. It looks good."

Vern tugs on a band of Reggie's hair until it straightens. He releases the lock and it bounces up, recoiling. "*You* look like somebody to reckon with. Got a tie. Shiny shoes. Fresh trousers."

"Naw. I should look fancy. But I look dull."

"Not to my eyes," Vern says.

The church doors crack open and a woman waves her quad cane. "Vernon? Let's go. Now."

Vern's face plummets. "It's my grandma. Gotta get to gettin'."

"Maybe I could meet her?"

Vern cranes his head and quickly says, "No, Reggie."

"Why not?"

The woman hollers, "Vernon? Let's go!"

"You don't wanna," he whispers.

"Sure I do."

"No."

"I bet she's great."

"Vernon! Come on, now!"

"I said *no!*" Vern's words are sharp, tinged with acid. "She don't like your kind."

Reggie watches him trot toward the exit. Then, Vern is gone.

Elmer's socks, his Stevie Wonder T-shirt, and a twelve pack of beer have all been zipped inside a blue suitcase, borrowed from Mrs. Lolly since he has never owned luggage.

Elmer folds up a letter for Pinky. He has, with fear, re-scrawled this several times. Again, he reads his words:

Dear Pinky,
Have a good trip. I'll be at Reggie's if you need to talk. The number is 978-534-8444.
Remember, if you feel scared, just think about something else like Christmas or an ice cream sundae or a funny joke. That's what I do. When we all get back, you and I can watch TV and I'll make a casserole. It will be fun. I promise. I'll miss you, Pinky.
I love you, Pinky.
I hope you believe me.
Elmer

He feels his blood patter when he reviews his closing admission. With fevered flesh, he slides the note beneath her door. He continues to repeat to himself, *Shit. Shit … Well, too late now. No, fuck it. Fuck it.*

Reggie Lauderdale steps over newspapers that choke the gutter. He walks on, then he stops, then he scrambles back, then he scrapes up the wet print, then he plunges it inside a garbage can.

Reggie strolls into Vic's Variety. He sees accordion turkeys, creamed corn, boxes of stuffing.

"Hey, Reginald." Vic is the only person who calls him this.
"Morning," Reggie replies.

Vic yanks his clip-on tie to the left. He dumps the *Give a Penny Take a Penny* cup into his shirt pocket. "How you been, kiddo?" he asks.

"Really pretty good, I have to say."

"Well, alright. Nice to hear. And what about your dad?"

"Same. He's the same. You know him."

"Heard he had some troubles."

"Yeah. His foot. He's on the mend, I think." Reggie says.

"Good. I never forget the Suzy Q's he likes. He's the only one in town who buys 'em so …"

"He'll be out and about soon. Dad can't resist sweets. Um … can I get ten scratch offs? Two dollar ones? Fast Cash? Please?"

Vic tears off tickets. He jabs the register, his eyes swivelling toward the yawning door. Maria. Her once dark tresses have been colored crimson. She cuts up to the counter, hips slapping, side to side.

"Maria. Hey," Reggie exclaims.

Vic almost hisses. "Here, Reginald. You owe me ten."

As Reggie unrolls his bills, he watches Maria glare at Vic. Vic asks her, "What *you* want?"

"No free coins?"

"None."

"That's a lie, Mister," she says.

"Do you see any?"

"You're hidin' 'em on me again? You always do."

Reggie clamps a hand on her shoulder. "Need a pop or something? My treat."

Vic says, "Nothing for *him*. Less *he* pays."

Maria scowls. "*I'm* a *she*."

"Right. In your dreams, freak."

Cussing in Spanish, Maria clomps out. "*Mama me la chocha.*"

Maria rests her heel atop the flaked fire hydrant. Pulling on a cigarette, she seethes. "Vic is an asshole, Reggie. Must have so much hate inside him."

"He's pretty nice to me."

"He's a fuck-face, honey. He's a meanie."

Reggie is scratching at each Fast Cash ticket with the hope of winning big. His card hollers: *15 CHANCES TO WIN, GET RICH NOW, $75,000 IN PRIZES.*

"Where's Elmer at?" Maria asks.

"Sleeping probably."

"With who?" She snakes about, her bangles clinking.

Reggie uncovers the final hidden number. He blows the silver dust away and gawps at his win. "Two dollars," he tells Maria.

"Big deal."

"Better than nothing."

"Know what I need? A man with big money. And a Ferrari. And a mansion. Maybe someone whose, like, eighty-three and ready to croak."

Reggie balks. "You're always talking about love, Maria."

"Right now I need money more than love."

"You say that love is unique. That's what you keep telling me. Right? Have you ever found it?"

"Sure. Here and there," she says.

"What?" Reggie asks. "You think love's too hard?"

"It's not *easy*. But I think all of us have got a dream boy or dream girl out there. Some place. Waiting for us."

"Really?"

"Absolutely. If one person isn't right ... *they isn't right*. They isn't your dream." Maria reaches out and strokes Reggie's earlobe. "Your dream will come true. And mine, too. Someday."

I know that Reggie longs to believe her, to believe his hopes will finally emerge. Soon. Tomorrow. By the holidays.

While his cousin bathes, Elmer Mott belches into the telephone receiver. Mrs. Lolly has already phoned three times.

She prattles on. "This place is a shit box, baby. My sister done makes me pray 'fore I eat *anything*. Even a single cashew. She asked me to come by for Thanksgiving too. No way. She's fuuuuucked."

"Your sister just wants you to be saved. *I* do too. We *all* do."

"Ha! Joker! The only thing they be savin' for me is a place in hell. I like it warm anyhow."

"You're satanic." Elmer searches for his cigarettes.

Mrs. Lolly squeaks, "I wanna go home, Elmer. I miss my brandy."

"One more day and then you can get plastered."

"Wonder how yo girl Pinky's doin'."

"She's fine. She's probably ... great." Elmer sighs and says, "I told her I'll miss her."

"That's real gentlemanly," Mrs. Lolly says.

"I told her I love her, too."

"Oh, lord."

"What's that mean?"

"Never thought you'd finally confess that one."

"Well ... I did. And I'm scared she'll flip out."

"Wanna know what *I* think?" Mrs. Lolly asks.

"Nope. No, thanks. Not really."

"Too bad, you little shit. I think Pinky'll jump right into your arms."

"I'm hanging up now," he shouts.

"Sweethearts, I say! Sweethearts!"

"Bye!"

Reggie yanks the clot of worn blankets away from his cousin. Again. Elmer is crooked up beside him.

Gentlemen Prefer Blondes plays. The picture casts out bands of rouge and white.

"I'm cold, Elmer," Reggie says.

"You're too grouchy for a slumber party." Reggie huffs and

says, "Why do you think that Vern would say that?" He huffs once more. "Vern said, 'your kind'. What kind am I? I don't get it."

"Um … I think he means the gay kind. He's a secret queer. The kid's in denial," Elmer replies.

"Maybe."

"Or he could be a wacko."

"But I thought Vern was … something else. I thought he liked me," Reggie says.

On screen, Marilyn oozes down a staircase, chaining herself in gobs of diamonds. She sings, *"Get that ice or else no dice."* "People don't make any sense," Elmer says and curls up tighter. "We're all retarded. But, if you want him, keep at it. Right?"

Reggie watches the Hollywood vixen shove away a man's offering of rhinestones. She quivers slowly, *"… you stand straight at Tiffany's …"* Reggie asks Elmer, "Want to pray with me?"

"No," he snaps. "That's annoying."

"Mind if I say my prayers out loud?"

"*Yes*. I mind. That's also annoying."

I see Reggie roll over. A landscape of barely blinking stars clog the window, like a cheap, faded mall painting. Like a fake, bootlegged sweatshirt. Beneath his breath, Reggie offers his thanks and gratitude, and gradually, forgets about his testicle.

I hear Reggie beg for just one thing.

I know that Elmer pictures Pinky buried beneath quilts.

I know that Elmer sees her, asleep and painless.

I know that Elmer envisions Pinky watching Pat Sajack.

I know that Elmer imagines her missing his jokes, his impressions.

I know that Elmer pictures her pills (probably the large orange ones).

I know that Elmer sees Pinky giggling.

I know that Elmer envisions her writhing beneath him.

I know that Elmer imagines thousands of possible days.

Reggie ambles to work. The town has finally chilled and a clean breeze tornadoes around him. Far inside his pocket, he is nudging through coins and receipts, attempting to squeeze his weary testicle.

Reggie silently prays, *Please make sure I'm okay. Please. And please make everything turn out alright.* Reggie peers upwards. He sees Vern waiting beside the church. He longs to turn away or disappear into an alley, but he walks on.

Vern says, "You think I'm a jerko now?"

Reggie hunches over. "Maybe."

"I quit the choir, ya know."

"*Why?*"

"'Cause of you."

Reggie exclaims, "I didn't do anything. Okay?"

Vern scratches his cheek and three pink stripes stain his skin. "My mama … back in Alabama, she sent me away. To this *place*. To make me change. And … it was … fuckin' torture. I had to make all this gone. I had to forget about that side of me. But you … you, Reg, you make me want."

"I want too."

Vern shoves Reggie, "I ain't gonna be this way. You're a faggot and *I* ain't gonna be one too."

Hulking red, oak parasols shade Elmer and his cousin. Elmer, booming with excitement, speed walks closer and closer to home. To Pinky. His pinstriped trousers are creased in manic, wrinkled tracks. He hurries—brims with jubilance—bumbles—watches speeding police cars—smokes another cigarette—tries to listen to Reggie.

Reggie explains, "Vern was … *mad*."

"He called you a faggot. Big deal. You *are* a faggot."

Reggie huffs. "Elmer. I don't like that word. The F word."

"It's not a curse for you, not now. It's like nigger. Black people can say that, 'cause they're black. You're gay so you can say faggot."

"I don't *want* to say it. No one should. It's mean. Just like the N word. And that's not what I'm getting at, okay? Vern thinks I'm, like, Lucifer or something. He thinks I'm terrible, awful. An abomination. Am I?"

"No, Reggie! Jesus. Vern's messed up. Forget him." Elmer spits his butt onto the curb.

"I don't want to forget him."

"What? You wanna marry him?"

Reggie, at last, is mute.

Elmer masks a bulging smile. Unseen balloons of thrill cluster inside him, clinging, swelling, romping, and he is unable to bat them away. Elmer will soon see Pinky. Soon, he will walk with her. He finally says, "I missed Pinky more than I thought I ever could."

Elmer enters Ninety-Nine Nixon Avenue. He coughs and says, "What the fuck is this?" A dense grey mist cloaks the lobby, feathering on all sides. Chemicals singe his eyes. Reggie hacks behind him.

A police officer tramples down the stairs, shaking his masked head. "Can I help you two sirs?" he asks.

"What's going on?" Elmer asks, wheezing. "I live here. What's the deal?"

"There's been an incident," the officer says.

"Can I move back in or what?"

"Well, which floor?" he asks. "We're waiting on some inspector"

"I'm on third." Elmer's eyes bleed tears.

"Oh, sure. Sure. Carry on." The officer shrugs. "Just open all your windows. Maybe go for a walk before bed."

A troupe of additional cops emerge, stamping upstairs.

Elmer asks, "What happened?"

"There was an accident." The officer grins. "Someone had an accident."

"Who?"

He binds his arms across his chest. "I don't think I can release that information. No. I don't believe I'm authorized to tell you."

Elmer asks, "Was it the girl? On the top floor? I know her."

"Ah, okay. Yes."

Elmer hacks. "Is she okay?"

"No. She found four insect foggers in the basement. Set them off. Took a permanent nap."

I see that Elmer now is nothing but an outline of a boy. He has been bleached of shine and detail. No features. No vibrancy. So very much has been erased.

All in just three minutes.

Cruisers cram the street. The blue lights skitter, gleaming from window to window.

A plaid-wearing woman hurries through the crowd.

Elmer watches her, recognizes her smile, even though he has never met her. Tears have sliced curvy lines through her makeup. "I'm sorry," is the only thing Elmer can say.

She grips her bag tighter and peers into space. She is wearing only one loop earring.

An ambulance suddenly shrieks, drowning out the world.

"I'm sorry!" Elmer exclaims again.

The woman, finally, faintly speaks. "I always knew today would come."

Elmer tells Reggie, "I said Pinky would be okay. But really, I knew it wasn't true. In my head. In my gut. I knew it wasn't true. I should have done something different."

Reggie replies, "You couldn't do anything. Nobody could."

"*I* could have."

"I don't think so."

Elmer's eyes gloss with grief.

"I'm sorry," Reggie says, "This is horrible."

Elmer asks, "Why would Pinky do this?"

"I guess that, um, she didn't know what else to do."
"She could have called ... she could have called," he cries.

⁂

Alone in his bedroom, Reggie prays, "Lord ... please take Pinky ... and hold her close ... because, I think, maybe ... only *you* can finally make her feel good or happy or okay. You know what I mean?"

⁂

Reggie says, "I'm going to win. I know it."
"You're a foolish boy," Maria tells him.
Snowflakes the size of bottle caps putter down from heaven like cinema snow.
Reggie cups four folded Shooting Star lotto tickets. The cards scream, *WIN! WIN! WIN! UP TO $1 MILLION IN PRIZES! YOU COULD BE A STAR!* He scratches. Scratches. Scratches. Scratches. Scratches. His winning numbers are twenty-two, one and eleven.
Maria stalks beside him, clad in faux fur and thrift store jewels. "So Pinky just murdered herself?" she asks.
"Suicide."
Maria swishes through the flurry of cold. "But why?"
Reggie continues to buff the tickets. "Pinky was off, you know. Sick. In her head."
"That's scary," Maria mumbles.
"And Elmer's a mess. He's not himself. He sleeps a lot more, drinks a lot more. He doesn't talk."
"Poor baby."
"I'm ... worried."
"He'll get better," Maria says, "We *all* mend."
"It's just ... he's hurting bad. *Real* bad. You know?"
Maria kicks off clumps of snow that cling to her heels.
Reggie says, "Nobody can make her come back. Nobody except God."

"Jesus Christ, honey. *He* can't even do that. When you're done, you're done."

Reggie spots the number. Eleven. Twenty-two. His brain deadlocks. He fails to breathe or move. Mini heaps of snow gather on his eyelashes.

Maria says, "Let's move. I'm freezin' my tits off, Reggie. And my hair's gonna be a nightmare."

Reggie's words are trapped. He checks and checks and checks the ticket.

"Walk and talk," she commands. "Walk."

"I won."

"How much?"

"I think, I think ... thirty-three thousand."

Reggie and Maria commence to riot through the white-out, yelping in full-pitched hysteria. The duo bound. Squeals, screeches. Children gawk.

"You're rich!" she yells.

"Oh my God!"

"Holy shit!"

Reggie gasps, "What will I do with it?"

"You could go to Tahiti ... or ... or the Virgin Islands."

"No, no."

"You could buy a car. A fancy race car."

"I don't need any of that." Reggie pets his face. "Maybe I'll give it to the church."

"Honey! No! You play those things every day."

"Yeah, but just for fun. I'd feel bad."

"Crazy boy!"

Reggie's hair and shoulders have turned white.

At two, Elmer prowled for coins, but found only a few pennies. At two-twenty, he urinated into an empty fast food cup. By three, shoeless, he tottered down to Mrs. Lolly's apartment.

Now, Mrs. Lolly peers through lacy curtains, complaining,

"Boy, it's a blizzard. What if we get snowed in? I ain't gonna have no drink. 'Cause you keep drinking it all!"

Elmer pours another sugar-canned cup. "I'll get you more," he says, flatly. "Promise. Cross my heart, hope to die."

Mrs. Lolly's living room is jammed with latch hook pillows. Furry lighthouse pillows. Flower and moonscape pillows. U.S. flag pillows. Elmer lifts a hound dog pillow and asks, "Where did you get all these?"

"I made 'em, boy. A dame's gotta have hobbies."

"I never, never, ever knew that about you." His face droops. "Elmer …"

"What?"

She softly says, "I talked to Pinky's mama 'fore she went. She left all her animals behind. Was gonna give 'em to the trash man, but Reggie thought you might wanna do somethin' else. Give 'em to little Jessie Smalls two streets over. Give 'em to the church."

He slurs, "Fuckin' Reggie."

In a tipsy cloud, Elmer craves to drown out the universe. All he wants to hear is the grumbling furnace in the basement. He longs for the hissing, the churning. He longs for the husky throttle. He longs for nothing else.

Mrs. Lolly says, "Give 'em to the kids! I think Reggie's got a fine idea."

"Whatever. Maybe."

She pats her wig. "Baby, you're hammered."

"I know."

Elmer gazes out Saran-wrapped window panes.

Mrs. Lolly says, "You ain't actin' so good."

"I'll be fine. Fine, fine, fine, fine, fine."

Elmer feels three knocks on his forehead.

Reggie begs, "Get up. Get up. Please?"

"No."

"You have to wake up. Mrs. Lolly is ready for bed."

"Leave me here," he says in a crusted voice.
"*No.*"
"Yes."
Elmer feels him knocking again.

Elmer, with airborne thoughts, says, "I ain't going to Pinky's place, Reggie!"

He shuffles on with smoky, blotted eyes. A week-old button shirt covers his back.

"Come *on*," Reggie tells him.

"No way."

Reggie jerks on his collar, tugging him up another step. "We're going to get the animals."

"I don't want to."

"Elmer! Just do what I fucking say! Okay?"

"Don't be so pushy. Better write that sin down, Reg."

The deadly fogger stench strangles Elmer. His eyes are tearing, his throat razorblading.

He helps Reggie round up the heap of elephants and unicorns and giraffes and ponies and bears. The plush zoo sits, abandoned on Pinky's bed. Elmer squeezes his jaw and says, "I told her the truth and she offed herself."

Reggie squints. "That's not why this happened."

"I probably freaked her out. I said, 'I love you' and it caused a mental split." He laughs maniacally. "I killed Pinky, Reg. I fuckin' killed her!"

"Don't be like this. You're scaring me."

Elmer plucks up a piglet and stares into its button eyes. "But I could be right. There's a chance. I might be a murderer."

Inside four basement dryers, creatures spin around, bonking one another. Tide axes through the room. Spring Scent. A nonstop hum vibrates around Elmer and Reggie as they sit, watching horses and hamsters hurtle.

Elmer wants to scream, *I need to sleep!* He wants to tell Reggie, *Fuck this shit.* But he can only sigh.

Reggie says, "I hit it big today."

"Ten bucks?"

"Thirty-three thousand."

"*Shut the fuck up.*"

"I'm rich."

"That's just ... perfect." Elmer strokes the trail of hair that loiters up toward his belly button.

Reggie says, "You see, anything can happen at any second. Sometimes awful things. Sometimes *terrific* things. So ... you won't *always* feel like this, not for the rest of your life."

Elmer drops a hand on his cousin's shoulder. He presses down, staring at Reggie's large, bedazzled eyes. "I don't want to hear it. Okay? I don't. I'm serious. And don't say 'terrific' ever, ever again."

"Okay," Reggie whispers, wilting.

Turning and turning. Turning ever more.

And, for now, I know that Elmer is gridlocked. I see him, unmoving, idling in a static haze of despair.

Gutted.

An hour ticks away. Some of the animals have damp heads, and others, hot paws. Elmer muscles the toys into plastic bags or closets or drawers or cupboards or boxes or cabinets or corners.

CHAPTER FOUR
FUCK GOD

It's mid-day at St. Leo's Church.

Reggie Lauderdale cleans the colourful, windowpane cherubs. His right hand is wrapped in wads of paper towel, like a bandage.

I watch him wipe away the grunge so new beautiful glows can penetrate.

"Hey ..."

Reggie wheels around.

Vern shivers. His nails are tipped in grime.

"Oh, hi," Reggie's face cramps "How you been?"

"Same as ever."

"You seem sort of ... *funny* today."

"Am I makin' jokes or some thang?"

"*No* ..."

Vern lunges. Reggie can smell the remains of a steak bomb submarine sandwich.

Vern asks, "You been wonderin' 'bout me?"

"A little bit."

"I've thought 'bout you too."

"Really?" he whispers.

"Yeah," Vern says and sighs.

"Like how?"

Vern tells him, "Look, I can't be no queer."

Reggie replies, "You know, I've felt just like you. For ... since ... *always*. But we were both made the same way."

"What about all them preachers? *Huh?*" Vern throws his hands skyward. "What about the bible?"

Reggie says, "They don't understand. I guess if the Lord didn't want us to be like this, he *wouldn't* have made us at all. And we can't change, not *really*, right?"

"But I want to. So bad. All the time. My brain's just screwy."

"Everyone's brains are screwy." Reggie holds back a laugh. "That's what Father Fink says."

Vern plops his head into his palms. "Sometimes, when I'm next to you, I can smile *real* smiles. And then, sometimes, I wanna rip myself apart."

Reggie's cheeks taper to a beat rose color.

Vern grabs Reggie's neck and jerks him near.

I find Reggie in sugared alarm.

And I watch the boys kiss.

Reggie's first kiss.

A real kiss.

Slight moans.

Tongues.

Lapping.

Swelled groins.

Sealed eyelids.

White snaps of light.

Joy.

Then, suddenly, Vern croaks, "I can't. No."

Reggie says, "It's okay."

"No. No."

"Vern …"

"*No.*" He wrenches away.

Reggie asks, "What? Everything's fine. I swear."

"It *aint.*"

"It is. It really is." Reggie reaches out and slowly strokes his forearm.

Vern's fist collides with Reggie's eye socket. His face shatters. Reggie is walloped again.

Reggie is mounted on the lectern, his mouth fish-hooked with fingers. He bucks. Something cleaves through his rear cavity. Peering up, Reggie can barely see the figure of Jesus Christ that bores down on him. The savior seems to grin.

Vern coughs, whispers, "Filthy faggot. Take it. Tell me how much you love this cock. Tell me how much you think about it … my dick knocking you up."

"*Don't …*"

"I know how bad you want this."

Reggie can feel Vern's penis drive inside him. His stomach smolders with fiery pangs. Blood coats his eyeballs.

Vern grunts. "I'll do his bidding."

Reggie, with a mouthful of pinkies and thumbs, whispers, "Why?" He struggles to say, "Stop," and "No." His face is slammed three more times.

I can see Father Fink beside the confessional box, groping himself.

Alone at church, Reggie's rear is wet. Warm. He feels as though he's been overstuffed. Reggie stirs and reaches behind. He pulls out quarters, a matchbook, crunched up bible verses, soggy hosts, his mother's rosary. Satin bands of blood seep from his anus. Reggie heaves.

Father Fink emerges. He swivels his head, to and fro.

Reggie asks, "Why?"

"I suppose … just … *because*."

"Why?" he caws. "Do you think I asked for it?"

Slowly, Father Fink replies, "Moments occur because, well, they're supposed to. Each and every thing has great meaning."

"What?" Reggie snivels.

"This could be a warning."

A shriek busts from Reggie, slicing the atmosphere. A cry to crack all kingdoms. He waddles away. Drops of gore and semen fall from Reggie's body.

A trail out.

Reggie Lauderdale's naked feet shave down the slushy, winter avenue. He does not consider his missing trousers, his orphaned pea coat. Reggie inhales with roaring sobs.

Reggie groans, collapsing through Elmer's door.

Elmer wanders from the bedroom in boxer shorts and a single sock. "Holy shit." He squats down. Elmer carefully pulls up Reggie's reddened briefs.

"Don't touch me!"

"What the fuck?! What happened?"

Faintly, Reggie whispers, "Vern …"

"Jesus Christ."

"It hurts so bad, Elmer," he sobs.

"I'm taking you to the emergency room."

"No! Dr. Dann said I can't."

"You're *going.*"

"*No!*"

Reggie is lifted up and lugged to the bathroom.

Reggie has been soaked in a hot, painful bath. He'd felt as though a hive of hornets stung his rear. His flesh is butterflied. He has been towel dried, fed four aspirin, and wrapped in a cocoon of blankets.

Now, he is slumped on the couch. "I knew I'd pay." Reggie proclaims.

I watch him in wide view, writhing in all this horrid muck that has just been birthed.

If only these events had not occurred in such a way.

Elmer can hear Mrs. Lolly call for him. He squashes out a cigarette—kicks on trousers—unplugs the radio—opens the door—cranes his head into the corridor.

"Elmerrrrrr? Elmerrrrrr?" Mrs. Lolly is poised beside the crowded mailboxes. Three giant curlers sit on her head like bright pink mini logs. She says, "I's been callin'. Don't ya answer yo phone?"

"Not so much. Probably off the hook anyway." Elmer's eyes spin backwards and a spunky grin spreads wide.

"Well, now ya get to see me lookin' all unladylike."

"You look gorgeous, Gorgeous."

Mrs. Lolly wrangles a Jet Magazine from her box. "I know what's been goin' on 'round here," she says,

"Oh really, Mrs. L?"

"These dang ceilings be too thin."

Elmer plunges a finger into his ear, which feels tacky.

She asks, "Is Reggie alright?"

"No."

"Thought so." She wags her head. "Look, boy. I'm 'bout to get tough on ya'. Reg don't got nothin' now. Not a *thang*. He ain't got no God. He ain't got no boyfriend. All he's got is you. You're grown. And right this second, he needs *you* more than anyone."

Elmer socks the papered wall. "What am I supposed to do, huh?"

"Save him," she replies.

"How?"

"Well … I don't know every *fuckin'* thang in the world. You figure it out for yo'self. But, just so ya know, I'm not askin' ya 'bout this. It's an order. Make things right. Understand?"

"Okay," he mutters,

Elmer Mott feels like he's tumbled down a well. He knows that he must, somehow, scale up and out. To hunt for all he longs to hunt. Elmer is sure he can find something, anything. And when he does, his days will shimmer once again.

I foresee that he can do much more than this. I am sure an infant world will soon be hatched.

See this.

Elmer watches his father. Mr. Mott is hunched over the kitchen sink, gulping from a Santa Claus mug.

"Dad?"

His father whirls around, winded with shock. "Jesus, Mary and Joseph!" he says. "God! You almost gave me a heart attack!"

"Sorry …"

He starts pointing. "Look, I got a question. Where's fucking Samson?"

Elmer releases a stuttering sigh. "I don't know. Whatever. Look. I want to drive for you now."

Mr. Mott laughs like a bottlecap firecracker. "You wanna do *what*?"

Elmer dims. "I want to drive."

"Really?"

He shrugs. "Yes."

"Look, I don't want you to half-ass this."

"I know," he replies, "I'm for real."

Mr. Mott grins. "Hey, well, that's great."

"Sure is."

"So … you came to your senses. Took a while, but you did. Finally."

"*Yeah.*"

I know that Elmer is nudged by sudden, internal, plummeting stabs.

Mr. Mott chuckles, "Everything's about to change. Wait till your mother hears about this."

Elmer stammers, "When do you want me to start?"

"Well, if *you* want, right after the Thanksgiving. Friday. Got a fella who needs a lift to the airport.

Elmer thumbs his belt loop. "Alright. I'm your guy."

Mr. Mott is airborne with pride. "I knew you'd listen. I knew you'd do the right thing."

Elmer watches his father radiate while he tops off his mug.

Elmer had phoned his mother, fibbing about a terrible bout of diarrhea. He longs to mask himself and hide away. Elmer is certain that Reggie feels the same.

I smell the turkey pot pies steaming before them and I watch their Thanksgiving.

Elmer tells Reggie, "Eat. I micro-waved these things for like, twenty minutes. They better be hot in the middle. Reggie pets his crushed, oozing, violet eye. "No wish bone this year, I guess."

Elmer says, "I still think you should go to the hospital. And we should call the cops …"

With a hint of venom, Reggie replies, "*Stop.*"

Elmer has never heard such a savage tone before. He is bulldozed. Elmer says, "Well, Vern shouldn't just get to walk."

Reggie slams both palms on the plastic tablecloth. "*Do not* tell *any*one. I don't care about all that. It's over."

Elmer stabs through his pie crust, slicing through the soupy insides. He glances at the clock. 11:11. "Look," he says. "It's time for a wish."

Reggie scowls at Elmer for seven curbed seconds. Finally, he laughs. "You know what I wish? I wish I was dead. I wish that Vern had killed me. But anyway, my wishes haven't *ever* come true. Now, I'm just … garbage."

Elmer rises. He pads over to Reggie and kneels at his side. "Am I a smart guy, cous?"

"Sometimes. Mostly."

"Am I your best friend? Am I like your brother?"

"Yes," Reggie replies.
"Would you vote for me?"
"Maybe."
Elmer asks, "Do you trust me? Do you *trust* me more than anyone in this world?"
"*Yes.*"
Elmer rests his hand on Reggie's scrawny thigh. "Then you have to believe what I say. You're a good guy. A *great* guy. You're fucking fantastic and there's *nothing* wrong with you. You're not evil. You're not a sinner. If you don't think I'm right … you don't love me. But I know you love me, 'cause I love you. So, in your mind, in your whole body, you have to know that what I say is true. You're Reggie … and Reggie is *stupendous*. Say you believe me. Say it."
I see Reggie wink his tears away. "I'll try and believe you, Elmer."
The cousins sink into a quiet timespace.
Elmer is made of anchors and anvils and he cannot move. His hand pushes down on his cousin.
Reggie repeats, "I will try." His purple eye glimmers.
Elmer huffs. "Everything's been so fucked up. Pinky. Vern. Our dads. The damn universe. But I have ideas. Maybe we can fix things. And, maybe, we'll turn out okay … okay?"

Reggie hammers his penis against his puckered skin. Slick. Sodden. He enters Jesus Christ.
Reggie asks, "How do I feel?"
"Heavenly."
He plunges deeply. "You want this. Don't you?"
"I need this."
Reggie drizzles cords of spit on Christ. "You're a whore."
"God …" Jesus whispers.
Reggie awakes, gorged in sadness. While the sun burns like a Mirabelle, he pulls off his briefs, swabs the semen, and plops a dab on his tongue.

Reggie Lauderdale watches Jesus Christ. The figure, with massive, outstretched arms, looks as though might applaud.

I am certain that Reggie craves to question countless things. He wonders, *Why did this happen? What is all this for? How can you be real, now?* Reggie, though, does not utter a single sentence. He merely stares and prays, "Dear God, I know that you're here, but what I don't know, is who you are anymore. The you I knew would never do this to me. I'm ... *furious*."

The confessional door sweeps open and Father Fink trips out gripping a cola. Smoothing his frock, he looks at Reggie and squints. "You look a mess, son."

"I know."

Father Fink says, "You'll be back to normal, well ... soon enough. Take it easy today. Not too much tidying."

Reggie exclaims, "I don't work here anymore."

"Ah ... *Ah* ... I see."

"I'm finished."

"Tell me about your ... *anger*. Tell me about your sadness. Let the Lord know."

"Forget the Lord. He's cruel."

Reggie watches Father Fink tug on his droopy jowls. "Without suffering there is no ..."

"I've suffered enough," he snaps.

"I don't think God sees things your way."

"Fuck God! Fuck Jesus! And fuck you too!"

The cassocked man steps back. "It's time for you to l eave, Reggie."

"I know."

Earlier, Reggie had flicked through the bible, slashing an X on each page with a magic-marker. Before that, he had shredded the Book of Revelation. And minutes ago, he had thrown away every prized wedding program.

Now, Reggie works the words that teeter and stumble from his tongue. "Mother fucker," he whispers. "Shit. Twat bag."

Reggie is slumped before the sink. He screws the H knob and whisks water. Blood begins to loosen from each rosary jewel. At this second, Reggie yearns for his mother's soothing head strokes and her long, long tales about Hollywood. And he questions if, maybe, his mother is simply rotting in the dirt, as Elmer would say.

I know that he is caged in a cold, metal room. All that Reggie once believed is scrambled.

A medley of chaos.

Mr. New President
1600 Pennsylvania Avenue NW
Washington, DC 20500

Dear Sir,

Greetings! It's me, Elmer Mott again.

Today, I'm really torn up about the justice system. No one should even call it that because is it truly just? Does it even work? Like really, really work? I don't think so. Murderers, rapists and crooks are everywhere. Freely. Some make careers out of being creeps. Do we need better police officers? And do we need laws that are no nonsense? What about punishments that are truly unfun? Like testing drugs and eye liner on criminals? Or, like, crazy shock therapy?

Listen, I might have some of my own answers. I'm just thinking about those dicks who never have to pay for their crimes. They're in justice debt!

I became a full-fledged taxpayer today, so I'm totally justified in saying, "SOMETHING SHOULD BE DONE!"

Feel free to let me know what you think of my ideas. Tell me yours too! Enjoy the day.

Sincerely,

Elmer Mott

Inside the limousine, Elmer feels like he is steering a parade float. He asks himself, *Aint that bad, right?* and *Why not?* Streetlamps burn above, each the color of a clean, polished penny. Elmer dials up the stereo and one of Maria's cassettes bawls. St. Leo's church sails by. He prods the brake pedal, slowing to thirty miles per hour, twenty miles per hour, fifteen miles per hour, five miles per hour. Elmer turns the wheel until his father's limousine purrs in front of the lumbering brick church.

Elmer enters. A grayish, lined man wobbles by, tipping his baseball cap.

Elmer can see a line of flickering candles. A crunched-up cola can. One used lottery ticket. He plucks up a bible and kneels before the lectern.

The limousine keys inside his front pocket mash against his thigh. He did not lock the doors. He had been told, by his father's firm voice, to simply drive to the airport by 9:00 A.M. But now, Elmer is dreaming of a trip to anyplace else. To the arcade. To Vic's Variety. To Atlantic City, as Pinky had wanted.

He sighs—fumbles for his Durels—flicks the lighter—torches the tip—puffs out portly smoke clouds. Elmer opens the bible and thumbs through the tissue-thin passages. Genesis. John. Moses. Peering up, he whispers, "Bullshit." His cigarette topples from the ledge of his lip, landing on page seventy-seven. Elmer watches a verse smolder. Each ancient word begins to blacken, to vanish. The flames leap up in a whoosh. He launches the bible and it collides with candles. Within the space of one commercial break, the helm of St. Leo's Church is an inferno. Flames slink up curtains, acrobating toward carved beams. Christ's left hand is ablaze.

Elmer backsteps away from the room of flare.

Elmer stampedes into the apartment, shouting for Reggie, "Hey! Hey! Where are you?" He wrings with panic, hotfooting from doorway to doorway. "Reggie!"

His cousin eases from the bathroom. Reggie cradles a blood-checkered hand towel. "What the hell?"

Elmer screams, "We've *got to go!*"

"Huh?"

"Get your lottery ticket and pack some clothes. Get all your shit. The cigarettes too, but DO NOT forget the ticket! Please!"

Reggie asks, "What the fuck is going on?"

"Listen to me!" Elmer launches both hands up into the air. "We *have* to leave!"

"Why?" Reggie reaches behind himself, rubbing.

"I did something ... *bad*."

"Like what?"

"St. Leo's. It's burning."

Reggie begins to yell, "What do you mean?"

"It's on fire!"

Reggie yells, "Shit!"

Elmer pounds the floor with his feet. "We need to fucking go. *Now!*"

I did watch Elmer drive to the state lottery claims office.

I did watch Elmer gather his T-shirts and unwashed intimates.

I did watch Elmer begging Reggie to pack his belongings too.

I did watch Elmer phone his father, saying, "I'm on my way back from job numero uno."

I did watch Elmer leave a case of raspberry brandy outside Mrs. Lolly's door.

I did watch Elmer load the limousine with all of Pinky's stuffed animals.

Elmer says, "We really *do* have to go, Reggie." He leans on the defrosting limousine.

"Is this the only way?"

"Well, yeah. What if they think *you* did it?"

"Why *me*?"

"You got raped. You quit. You bitched out the boss."

Reggie says, "What about our parents?"

"We're gonna have to leave them. Your dad ... he'll have to take care of himself ... for once. We'll have to forget *everyone*. At least for now."

Reggie asks, "We don't have another choice?" He yanks on a handful of curls.

"Look ... I can't come up with anything else."

"Where are we going to go?"

Elmer proclaims, "To Aunt Dolly's, I've decided."

CHAPTER FIVE
NEW

Reggie Lauderdale slumps, cozied inside the limousine. He is nuzzled by ponies and bears, Pinky's animals practically devouring him. Reggie watches the town haze by. Vic's Variety, City Hall, a school, a cemetery, Cool Car Wash, a strutting Maria.

"Pull over!"

"Fuck!" Elmer shouts, stomping on the brake pedal.

Reggie lunges forward as the luxury car grinds to a halt. He presses a button and the blacked-out window descends. He yells, "Maria! Hey!"

She spins around, her fur coat cruising, twirling through the frigid air. Spooked, Maria clicks over to the car. "Reggie? Honey? What happened to your face?"

"Well, shit happened, I guess."

"*Jesus* ..." she says.

Reggie roots through a grocery bag and yanks out almost five-thousand dollars. He shoves the cash toward her. "Take this. For your operation. Just to, sort of, get you started."

"*No*," she replies.

"Yes."

"You play those cards every day. *You* won it. The jackpot is yours."

Elmer cranes his head out into the cold. "Listen to Reg, beautiful."

Reggie tells her, "You *have* to have it. It's meant for *you*."

"I won't," she says, hissy fitting on the sidewalk. "*Honey* ..."

"Come on, Maria. It's an early Christmas present. That's all."

"You sure?"

"*Yes.*"

Maria squeezes Reggie's hand. Squeezes harder still. "You're an angel."

"Right."

Maria takes his money, squashes the mess of bills against her flat chest.

Elmer yells, "Time to move!"

"Chicos?" Maria asks, "How you ridin' in such glamour?"

Elmer says, "We're the *new* Reggie and the *new* Elmer."

"But where you speedin' off to? You're comin' back, si?"

"Doubt it," Reggie tells her.

"No?"

"Time to go!" Elmer commands again,

Maria says, "Thank yoooou."

Reggie sees pearls of sadness mess her mascara as they hustle off, fishtailing through the snow.

Fourteen suns have climbed toward heaven.

Reggie continues to bleed. At rest stops he unzips his trousers and removes bundles of warm, bloody tissue. But Elmer told him to toss his garbage out the window and Reggie gratefully complied. Several days ago he heaved the bloodiest clump yet, which didn't go far and stuck to the side of the vehicle. "Uh oh," Reggie exclaimed. Elmer stopped the limousine. He swatted it off with a stray branch.

Still, I can see that Reggie heals a little more each day.

Better, better.

His old life has been completely carved away. Now, Reggie feels as though he is living, shadowboxed. He remains sealed inside a cube, looking out through a pane of dim, faux glass. Watching life unfold.

Outside.

Elmer curses the spiking temperatures that smack the south. Heat squiggles up from the asphalt. He has just cruised across another state line. Elmer hasn't spoken to Reggie for almost two and half hours because, in truth, he has no words to offer. Many miles before, Elmer had turned to his cousin and said, "We'll be friggin' fine." That was all he could manage. Elmer hoped he was right. They *would* be fine.

I know that, roving toward a strange newness, Elmer struggles to ignore his manic spree of thoughts. He thwarts cell mate scenes, mess hall scenes, prison yard scenes. I hear Elmer brush away the fear that broils inside his head. Shanks. Freezing silver toilet seats. Olive loaf lunches.

All Elmer can do is drive and striveand vanish inside the black hole of pop songs that quake around him.

Elmer reeks of flimsy, motor lodge soap. Because of his cousin's bellyaching, they have stopped for countless nights. The Thunderbird Motel and the Concord Lodge. The Franklin Hotel and the Easy Inn. Many others, too.

Elmer's eyes now trace their current room. He half-counts the blotchy stains that mar the rug. He sees a rotary telephone and a bed and wooden lamps and endless paneling and a snowy layer of dust that blanches everything in sight.

Reggie elbows by, balancing a stack of Styrofoam containers. "Where *are* we?"

Elmer says, "I don't know. I forget. Whatever. Let's eat before I die."

Elmer is sprawled on the queen-sized bed. He swabs a French fry bouquet with tartar sauce and joyfully devours their food.

Reggie sighs, "Tartar sauce? Who *does* that?"

"*Me*. I do." Elmer says. "And it's good. You should try it."
"No way."
"It's the best."
"Gross."

Elmer watches Reggie fork a tray of browned, popcorn shrimp. Elmer notes that Reggie's eye remains purple and gold, but can almost completely open. "Your face looks better, cous."

Reggie quickly says, "I'm ugly."
"Zip it."
Reggie asks, "What are we gonna do when we get to Aunt Dolly's?"
"We'll see what happens."
"What if nothing happens?"
"Hey … something will," Elmer explains. "Something always does."

Reggie asks, "What if Dolly doesn't want us around?"
"She won't even know. Dolly and Herb travel the globe. They only return to Jupiter every third Christmas. They were here last year, so it's one big empty place." Elmer dunks more fries and droplets of tartar plummet to the bedspread. "It can be our little hideout, for now."

Reggie pokes at his swelled, bubbling torso. He says, "This take-out is making my stomach flop around." Reggie switches the lamp on, which flickers, snaps, and implodes. Dead.

I know that Reggie Lauderdale has been considering the sins he once deemed illicit.

Curses.
Vanity.
Cocktail hour.
Kissing.
Dirty jokes.
Cineplex moans.
Kissing.

Touching.

Reggie has never reached out to this universe because he was always taught from one single touch, he would ignite. Now, though, Reggie asks himself, *What is really wrong?*

As a fitness commercial plays, he tells his cousin, "Give me one of your beers. Please."

"You don't drink, Reg."

"I do today."

Elmer snaps open a Meister Brau and it erupts with fizz. He passes the can to Reggie, "You're unbelievable."

Reggie tips back the brew, sucking. "The bubbles are, like, scraping my throat."

"Super," Elmer says. "Just don't get out of control."

"What? I'm fine. Everything's fine. Because like you said, we're the *new* Reggie and the *new* Elmer."

Reggie wrings in a filmy luster. "I get why you drink all the time."

His cousin replies, "Oh, yeah?"

"Yeah. *Yeah.*" Reggie dwells on this proclamation. His eyes swivel toward the ceiling. "Everything is …"

"Better?"

"Yes!" Reggie shouts. "And everything's fun, and, like, um, fluffy, and, you know, different."

"You're plastered and you're going to barf everywhere. I just know it." Elmer says.

"I will not," Reggie replies. He crumbles into comedy.

"You'll be hugging the bowl tonight."

Reggie wrestles around, shoving pillows to the floor. "Booze is magnificent," he sings in soprano. "Because booze makes you feel great … or nothing at all."

"Sometimes it's like that. Yeah."

"Elmer? When are we going to get to Jupiter?"

"Soon … if we quit stopping all the time."

"Like the planet, right? We're going to fucking outer space!"

I haven't, in thirty days, seen Reggie Lauderdale simmer with so much glee. Because he appears a little brighter, the boys stay on for seven more sunrises.

It is the eve of Christmas.

Elmer pops the blinker skyward, turning left. He remembers the morning of each December twenty-fifth, when his stocking lay on the love seat sofa. Elmer's mother would pack it with deodorant or socks or Durels or boxer shorts or chewing gum.

This year, marooned in a curious place, he hankers for a stocking stuffed with hope.

Elmer sees that the municipal airport is slack, barren, and hushed, as if someone has called for a moment of silence, yet not for refrain. Elmer beaches the limousine beside two rubbled runways. He leads Reggie inside the Pilot's Diner, saying, "This is the only place I could find," and "At least they have slaw," and "See... they've got beer on tap."

Inside the eatery, a fleet of model aircrafts teeter and spin from the cork ceiling. Elmer sees supersonic jets, red barons, helicopters, hot air balloons. The miniatures weave from ceiling fan turbulence. Wings shift, propellers spin.

"I'm starved, cous," Elmer says.

"Is this real or fake?"

"Who cares? Let's eat."

I watch them plop down at the counter, open hand-printed menus.

Elmer says, "Look. The Number Six Special. Franks and beans. Your favorite."

"I think this might be the weirdest place in the world," Reggie tells him.

"No shit," Elmer replies.

A waitress stalks out from the kitchen. Cigarette smoke trails behind her. With burgundy lips and dark locks, she waves. "You two are out late. If you don't get on home and go to sleep, Santa won't show up." She laughs. "But … I need the tips, so you *gotta* stay."

Elmer stares at the waitress for seven long seconds.

She says, "I can tell that you recognize me."

Elmer is clueless. "Yeah."

"From the news. Years ago. I was the weather gal." "She tells them,." "Sometimes, I covered special, human-interest stories too. Those were my best segments."

Elmer hacks up grit from his throat and exclaims, "Of course."

"I'm Laurie Fooz. And thanks to poor representation and black tar heroin, I'll be your waitress tonight."

Elmer asks, "I don't mean to be a dick, or anything, but this place seems a little … *off*."

"Oh, yes." She plants both hands on her hips. "Just an ancient, local airport. Private pilots. I don't think they've even got guys in that stupid tower. But we're open all day, every day. Banner flights and advertising crud. If you ask me, though, they're flying in drugs. Coke, probably."

Elmer asks, "How do you know?"

"Just a guess. The only incoming flight tonight is at eleven p.m. Always the same guys. Real skinny. Like beans. And they only order Pepsi. Great tippers, though."

Elmer sees a plastic Santa slouching beside a coffee pot. "I guess I'll have a Number Seven Special," he says.

"Sloppy Joe, huh?" she says. "Hmmm. Why don't they call it a Sloppy Sam or a Sloppy John? Maybe Joe was a wreck. Most guys are sloppy. Ladies too. We're all a little messy, right?"

"Right," Elmer says.

Elmer swallows the last bite of shredded meat. "Not friggin' bad," he says.

Reggie aims his knife at four cubes of lard resting on his plate. He tells Elmer, "Here. Take these. I know you love them."

Elmer scoops up the fat. "Best part."

"Well, Merry Christmas!"

Elmer grins at his cousin and slips the treats onto his tongue.

Laurie Fooz swishes in from out back. She smiles as if camera lights still beam. "Was it delectable?" she asks.

"Absolutely," Elmer says, wiping his lips.

"Coffee?"

"No, thank you," Elmer replies.

"So, why you boys out on Jesus' birthday, anyhow?" She slides the twelve dollar and twelve cent check across the counter.

Elmer explains, "I guess you could say we got no other place to be."

"Me either, I guess. 'cept here." She giggles. "Fuck crappy presents and eggnog."

With a tiny stroke of wistfulness, Reggie reveals, "I think it's nice. Being here. Right now. It feels good."

Laurie Fooz turns to the right, posing more. "I'll bag up some brownies for you boys."

Later, following a loud, relentless bowel movement, Elmer leaves Laurie Fooz a one-hundred-dollar tip.

Reggie craves a Christmas scene: Jumbo bulbs with garlands and Brenda Lee records and tinsel and snowflake cookies. Reggie also longs to hear his father's voice. While Elmer scrubs insects from the windshield, Reggie plucks up a graffitied telephone. He dials.

"Dad?"

Instantly, Mr. Lauderdale is screeching, grumbling. "Where in Christ are you?!"

"I can't say."

"Tell me!" he shouts.

"I won't."

"Is your messed-up cousin tagging along?"

"No."

"That means yes. Did Elmer torch St. Leo's Church? That's what *I* think. That's what most people think. And his father's 'bout to have another heart attack."

"Dad?"

Mr. Lauderdale becomes silent.

"Dad?"

"What, Reggie?"

"I just want to say, Merry Christmas."

"Not so damn merry, don't you think?" he says.

Inside Reggie, something foreign swells like a party balloon, and the favor quickly explodes. "I know, dad! Everything's fucked up and we're trying to fix it. Jesus Christ!"

His father gasps.

"If you love me, if you *ever* loved mom, you won't tell on us. Please say you'll stay quiet about this."

Mr. Lauderdale sighs. "I *ain't* proud. I *ain't* pleased … but I'm no Grim Reaper."

"Goodbye, dad."

Reggie Lauderdale hobbles toward Elmer, blue runway lamps rimming his path. He breaks the lull and proclaims, "You know, this is all unbelievable. Us. Here. Now."

Elmer sneezes, hacks and spits out a clump of snot.

"That's *real* nice," Reggie says.

"Hey, I'm a classy guy."

"I think I feel … better," Reggie tells him.

Elmer laughs. "Well, *I* don't. I feel like we're about to get in trouble. Like me and you are going to get busted at any minute. The cops. *Everything*. We're fucked."

Reggie is staring at the murky, lavender sky. "But what if everything's okay? What if *we're* okay? What if everything is exactly how it's supposed to be? And I've decided, that I really am someone new. I don't know what that means, I guess. But I want you to be new too."

Elmer replies, "Well, fuck it. We'll see."

"Thanks for trying to make things better."

"Didn't really have a choice, right?"

I see their cheeks, t-shirts and eyelids are cast in dark blue.

Reggie tells him, "Give me a hug."

Elmer shrinks. "Now?"

"Yes. Don't be a dick-face."

Reggie feels Elmer'scousins' arms loop around him. His doughy gut. His prickled cheek. A soft embrace.

Reggie commands, "No. A *real* hug. Use your muscles."

"Alright. Fine. Don't get a boner or anything."

Reggie feels him clutch harder. Tighter.

I know this is real.

Sonic rumbles crack and throttle above. I watch as they peer up toward the wobbling lights of a small plane, dipping and skidding over the runway.

Both cousins choke on laughter.

Elmer steers toward Jupiter. He does not allow the speedometer to rise above fifty miles per hour. His eyes regularly lock on each mirror, scouting police.

As he coasts by exit 44A, Elmer sees two large domes up ahead, their summits kissing the clouds. Everything blurs by: Towers and then, gates and then, ponds of green foam and then, more gates, and then, large caution signs and then, more caution signs. A constant, feeble hum carpets the landscape.

Elmer hears Reggie ask, "What is all this?"

"It's a nuclear power plant. A fucking big one. Jesus."

Reggie replies, "It's crazy what people can build if they want to. Or have to. I guess we all need our TVs and microwaves to work, huh?"

Elmer spots another sign, dented and sun-bleached, "JUPITER 53 MILES." Parading by, he pretends not to notice a flock of seagulls by the roadside, rotting in an emerald pool.

Reggie is pestered by the light. A quarter moon beams, synthetic, unreal, film-like. He sees that the limousine's clock broadcast the time. 2:22 A.M. If he chooses to make a wish, Reggie believes his hopes might multiply, grandly. If he still believes.

With muted fancy, he quietly begs the universe. "I wish for two wishes. First ... a million more wishes. Second ... to live the high life. Like they do in Saturday afternoon flicks."

I see Elmer imagine a cyclone of police lights.
I see Elmer predict a ten-cruiser highway chase.
I see Elmer envision the jurors.
I see Elmer imagine a prison cell with initialed walls.
I see Elmer predict dinners made from ground meat, carrots and blocks of corn bread.
I see Elmer envision quick showers.
I see Elmer imagine himself trapped for only one accident, one secret.

Exit 6 is drawing close. Jupiter.
Reggie rolls down his window and sea scents whip his face. "Is this it?" he asks Elmer.
"That's what the map says."
Reggie leans over the front seat. Half-thrilled, he kills the air conditioning and opens every window. The sunroof too.

Reggie feels the limousine putter up the crimson, pebbled driveway, like a long red carpet of crushed glass. He can hear the tires spitting up stones, digging up sand, until they finally reach the estate. Reggie exclaims, "Jesus, I mean wow. I never knew their house was this … big."

Elmer tells him, "Dolly and Herb are completely loaded. Lucky ducks."

Reggie's eyes swallow the sights. A giant fountain spurts in the courtyard. He counts thirty shuttered windows. He sees vast etched pillars, he sees iron statues, he sees five stories, he sees countless faux Christmas wreaths, he sees lemon trees, he sees two ceramic Santa's guarding the doorway. Reggie says, "How are we going to get in?"

Elmer attempts to jolt his memory. He asks himself, *Where is that fucking house key? Beneath garden stones, or by palms, or above the back door?* But none are correct. Still, he prowls, peeping spot to spot.

Reggie leans against the fountain, "What are we going to do, Elmer?"

"I thought I knew where it was. Gotta be around here somewhere."

"This is *perfect*. Are we going to break in?"

I watch Elmer flash his cousin a wry look. He sits beside Reggie, nudging him, twice.

Elmer exclaims, "Why don't you help me find it, then?"

Reggie pitches a half-smoked cigarette into the fountain. "Jesus. Maybe we should just go home."

Droplets of water cool Elmer's neck. He begins to squash his head and the heaviness inside bops around. "We'll work it out," Elmer says. "We'll find the key. I promise."

Reggie says, "Maybe this is all … I don't know, a sign?"

"Jupiter is right. I'm sure of it." Elmer turns to see his cousin staring into the fountain water. The zinging reflection of drowned coins blazes up at them.

Reggie laughs. "Maria would have a field day here. She'd grab *all* those quarters and dimes." He grins. "Pennies too."

Elmer tells him, "Looks like a lot of folks made a lot of wishes. My mom told me that Dolly used to have some real whacked out parties with all the show biz lot. Don Ho, Sinatra. That could be their money. Famous money."

"Did you check the welcome mat? Everybody hides keys there."

"That's too obvious, Reg. That's like asking for crooks to bust in."

"So, you *didn't* check there?"

"No," Elmer replies. "That's a lame spot."

Reggie asks, "Are you *going* to check there?"

"That's probably the fucking place, right?"

"Um ... maybe." Reggie lights another cigarette.

Elmer chuckles and gazes into the water. Among the glittering coinage, he spots a splotch.

The key.

He leaps in, loafers and all. "I got it. I got it!" He shouts amid splashes.

Reggie laughs. "Ridiculous."

The piping gush of water drenches Elmer. "Alright," he spits. "Call me a doofus. I'm a fucking doofus."

"You're a lucky fucking doofus, Elmer."

"Ha!"

Reggie Lauderdale eases inside, past Elmer. Reggie's eyes snapshot every detail. Frosted chandeliers. Carpets. Gold-trimmed stockings. Sofas. A giant plastic Christmas tree. Two long staircases. A half-full candy dish. Waxed bunches of mistletoe. Holly. See-through nutcracker soldiers. Bows. Gossamer drapes. A wall of vintage records. Speakers. Stray tinsel. Reggie also sees a diamond bracelet snaked on an end table.

Reggie stirs, pinches the jewelry and lays it over his wrist.

Elmer asks, "What you got?"

"It's a tennis bracelet, I guess. Think Dolly would mind if I borrowed it?"

Elmer balks, "You don't even know how to play tennis."

"Doesn't matter," he says, fixing the clasp. "Jerk."

"You're getting feisty, Reg."

"True." Reggie smiles.

Reggie tells Elmer, "They have a Christmas tree in every room. And so many decorations. They're everywhere. Why didn't they take them down?"

"Don't want to go through the trouble, I guess. I don't know." Elmer replies,

Craning his head, Reggie spots the pool, which is shaped like a lower-case t. "Come look, Elmer," he says, rushing out to the patio.

I watch Elmer follow. Both cousins gaze at the babbling body of water.

"It's so nice," Reggie coos.

"Swanky," Elmer replies, rubbing his gut. "We're here, Reg. Now what are we supposed to do? We going to grow stupid moustaches? Get fake I.D.'s? Work at the strip mall? You know, that money won't last forever."

Reggie blinks away sun beams. "Elmer ... ever since I was, like, two, I've always worried about what's coming next. What's coming tomorrow? Death, damnation. But I don't have to worry about any of that now."

"We have to figure some shit out."

Reggie grins. "I say, *fuck it*. Have fun. Why not, right? What else can we do?"

"So, we just have fun?" Elmer asks.

"Yeah. For now. As much fun as we can."

"Okay," he says, smirking.

Reggie feels Elmer's hand collide with his collarbone and he's soon airborne off the pool's edge. He belly flops into the warmth.

Underwater, Reggie thrusts open his eyes. He is buried in a bright bubble storm. Quiet and calm. No noise or nuisance. No worry. No pressure grinding down on him. Eventually Reggie emerges, sputtering, tittering, flailing. He hollers, "Asshole!"

"You having fun yet?" Elmer asks.

Reggie splashes his cousin. "Get in!"

CHAPTER SIX
EL PRESIDENTE

MICHAEL GRAVES

PARADE

MICHAEL GRAVES

PARADE

MICHAEL GRAVES

PARADE

MICHAEL GRAVES

PARADE

MICHAEL GRAVES

PARADE

MICHAEL GRAVES

PARADE

MICHAEL GRAVES

PARADE

CHAPTER SEVEN
THE COOKBOOK

Reggie Lauderdale is packed with voltage, longing to write the truth. He raids through kitchen drawers searching for spare paper and pens? Reggie discovers matchbooks and plastic cutlery and receipts and orphaned bolts and lint and Christmas gift tags. Eventually he unearths a bouquet of pens.

Reggie sighs and tramps upstairs to the red bedroom. He plops down at the vanity, yanks open a drawer and sees a tin recipe box. Reggie tells himself, *No. Dolly never cooked anything. She hired caterers.* Inside, he finds countless blank cards. Reggie now has paper. Reggie now has ink. His innards jounce and rattle. He begins to write.

Betterment
Time.
Cruelty.
Manners.
Work.
Beauty.
Goodness.
Right now.
I watch while Reggie Lauderdale scrawls.
The truth inside himself.

RECIPE #1

You should be good. I do not mean good at your job. I do not mean good-looking. You must be good to the people around you.

Say, "hello." Let strangers pass before you. Say, "thank you." Give someone your last root beer sucker. Say, "excuse me." Hold the door open for another. Say, "please." Allow someone to use the lavatory first. Say, "good day." Lug a lady's grocery sacks to her automobile. Say, "good evening." Shovel the snow from your neighbor's walkway.

My suggestions could go on for countless cards. But you understand. Just BE GOOD.

Goodness always multiplies. It will lighten us all.

So, just try it, okay?

RECIPE #8

You feel things. I do too. Sad. Happy. Confused. Frustrated. Everyone feels. Be honest about these feelings. It's tricky, but you must.

If you feel lonely, just say so. If you're jubilant, tell someone. Maybe you're furious; explain. You may be scared; scream about it!

Once you state your feelings, you'll feel a whole lot better. Everything is released. Others will know your truth. And you will be real.

Why hide your feelings? Everything else is a waste of time.

RECIPE #21

Stop lying. Lies are hideouts.

If you fouled up, caused a fender bender, come clean. If you gossiped unkindly, tell those involved. If you piddled on the toilet seat, admit it.

When you have secrets stashed away? They will only press on your heart. And don't believe in little lies either. It's silly. What's the point?

Remember, if you are honest, you are FREE.

Reggie stirs his cocktail with a pen.

He asks himself, *Recipes?* Reggie wonders, *How can this even matter?* He asks himself, "Who really cares?" He wonders, *How will this change anything?* Reggie sighs, battering a band of doubt. These truths begin to feel like ancient coupons. Or dopey one-liners.

I watch as Reggie Lauderdale reluctantly resumes to write.

Poolside, Reggie hands Reverend Rockwell a batch of recipes. And a Margarita. He says, "Here's my homework. Like you said, I wrote stuff down."

The man skims a recipe, pulls on his pink straw, skims another.

"Sorry, I couldn't find a notebook." Reggie says.

"Oh, no worries, son." He pats his knee.

Reverend Rockwell sighs and squeezes his rumpled forehead.

"It's stupid, right? Dumb?"

"Oh, no … this is just right."

"You sure?"

Reverend Rockwell stamps his feet. He laughs like a toddler. Sips some more. "You're getting down to it. You're getting it done!"

"Really?"

I see smears of ink on Reggie's cheek, Reggie's nose, Reggie's eyelid. His pen has exploded, but he has not yet realized.

I see he has found a flurry of rapture. I see him bloat with a deluxe newness.

I am certain he cannot cease.

Reggie is perched at the neon bar, penning more recipes when a strange girl skips in. Reggie's face crinkles.

She is dressed in only panties. She hums and reaches for a half-drunk bottle of whiskey.

Reggie says, "Um, hi there."

She startles and twirls around. "Oh. Shit. You scared the fuck out of me. Are you Reggie?"

"Yeah."

She quickly covers her bare breasts. "Oh … oops. Are you okay with bosoms?"

Reggie is dumbed by this brash, wild stranger. "I don't know," he says. "I'm gay, so …"

Her arms limply fall away. "Oh. I love gay guys. They're the best. "She titters.

"What are you doing here?" he asks.

"Sorry. Yeah. I fucked your cousin. He's *sooo* cute. I'm Polly."

Reggie glugs his cocktail.

"Elmer's not like everyone else. He's … he's funny … sweet. He's kind of … old-fashioned. Does that sound weird?"

"I guess not."

Polly asks, "Got any ginger ale around here? I'm going to make high balls for everyone!" She places three mugs on the bar.

Reggie lobs his head to the side. "No thanks. Not me."

"Oh … I meant for me, my sister and Elmer. But if you want one too …"

"Your sister's up there?"

Recipe #24
It's easy to become jealous of others. I know.

Sometimes, people have more than you. Nicer hair-dos. Bigger houses. More lovers. Beautiful children. Loads of money. Maybe they have perfect jobs or perfect husbands or perfect Porsches.

And I hope they're content. Right?

So, instead of being jealous, try celebrating them. Clap. Cheer. They have some form of fortune. And why shouldn't they?

So … try feeling happy for people. Then, I think you'll feel happier too.

Reggie weaves through the garden pools that pack Reverend Rockwell's estate. He eyes waterfalls and red-striped fish and spurts of grass and arbors and a giant bullfrog. Reggie squints through sprays of sunlight and pokes the doorbell. Reverend Rockwell appears.

"Hi, Reverend."

"Reggie! Hello! Howdy!" He speaks as if his throat is rollercoasting. "Good day! Good afternoon! Buenos tardes!"

A moth flits before Reggie's face. He reaches out and traps it. Squashes the creature.

Reverend Rockwell says, "Be kind to all things. Even bugs. They have a soul too."

Reggie shrugs. "Really?"

"Yes. Of course. That's why I don't eat animals. It's not very kind. Ponder that, maybe."

"I never really thought about it."

"Then you should. No? Yes, you should, you should."

"I will. So ... are you, like, busy?" Reggie asks.

"'Course not, son. I'm delighted to see you. What's on your mind?"

Reggie hands over a tin of twice-written recipes. "A few more. If you could take a look."

"Wonderful," he exclaims, accepting the box. "This is just ... stellar." Reverend Rockwell snorts, laughing loud.

"I started and couldn't stop." Reggie peers at Reverend Rockwell, "Are you okay? Are you alright?"

The Reverend snorts again. "I'm perfect, son. And so are you."

I see Reggie half-grin. "Right."

Elmer has mixed two beverages. A sidecar and a bubblebath. Elmer has also prepared a platter of cheese cubes and walnuts. He recalls key passages from *The Bartender's Manual,* one of which stated fine entertaining not only concerns spirits, but thoughtful appetizers as well. Elmer tells Reggie, "My research is finished! Here. Try this. A sample of your signature drink."

"What is it?"

"A sidecar."

"What's a sidecar?"

"It's a *drink*. Duh. It's also a little extra compartment you can hook onto a motorcycle. A girlfriend ... or a boyfriend, could ride in it."

Reggie indulges and instantly his face contorts. "No. *No*. Not my drink. And I don't wanna ride in somebody's sidecar anyway. I need my own car."

Elmer passes him the bubblebath, "You haven't said shit to me in days. What's up your poop shoot?"

Reggie flusters. "Well ... what are you up to, Elmer?" He whispers, "You're f-ing two girls? And sisters?"

"Don't be so touchy. They're harmless."

"And will they ever go home?" Reggie asks. Elmer jousts the air with a frilled toothpick. "Don't forget. We're the *new* Reggie and the *new* Elmer. So ... *be new*." Elmer buries the pick between his rear molars.

"Hey, I'm trying. Sorry." Reggie slugs back the second drink. "Mmmm. What's this one called?"

"A bubblebath."

"It's fizzy ... and sweet. It's not terrible. It tastes like candy, sort of."

"Told you I was an expert."

"*This* is my drink! The bubblebath." Reggie smiles.

"Fucking spectacular." Elmer sneers and pitches a cashew at his cousin.

"Hey!"

"Don't be an ass about what I do. You and I, we put the past away right?"

"I suppose."

Elmer locks his hands inside his armpits. "Then don't judge me. Everything's okay. Okay?"

Reggie swipes at his forehead. "Okay."

"You've got your recipes. You're making up your own rules. So am I, Reg."

"Alright, Elmer."

RECIPE #16

Don't judge others. This can be trying, I know. Judgment is a reflex, like when the doctor taps your knee with a hammer. But you must fight the urge!

Don't judge how people act, or how they look or speak. Don't judge what others believe.

We're all so different. We're all so unalike. And that is beautiful. We are beautiful. All of us. Life would be a bore if we were all the same.

So, don't do it. You don't judge me. I don't judge you.

All is even. All is fair.

I watch every day.

The dolls only depart to bathe and re-dress in spangled couture frocks. They steal away as Elmer sleeps and return before he rouses. It has been close to a month since they met. He ejaculates four times a day, at least.

Elmer reclines on the patio in one of Herb's porkpie hats. His potbelly has become brown. He passes Polly his cigarette. "I keep telling you. I'll buy you a pack of your own."

Polly inhales, smoothing her lemon-colored gown. "I don't smoke."

Elmer turns to Doris who is staring at Reggie scribbling on recipe cards.

Doris asks, "What exactly are you plotting, Mr. Lauderdale?"

Reggie scoffs, "Nothing."

Polly interjects, "Are you writing secrets? Dirty secrets?"

"Or the great American novel?" Doris says.

Elmer cackles, "Leave him be for Christ's sake. He's writing a cookbook. A Godly one. A cookbook bible."

Doris stirs. "Sounds compelling."

Drunkenly, Elmer says, "He's a fucking savior. He's gonna rescue the whole damn world!"

Doris doesn't blink. "Well, why not. The old bible can't help any of us now. Someone really should say something new."

Reggie says, "It's just … ideas."

"Ideas about what?" she asks.

"Ideas … about life … It's a bit of fun. Our neighbor and I have just been messing around."

Elmer says, "The guy next door used to be a preacher on TV."

Doris sweeps a curl away from her cheek. "Can I steal a peek?"

"No," Reggie says. "It's private."

"Well, I think it's tremendous." Doris replies. "You have some sort of goal. You have some sort of objective. I wish I knew what my plans are. Being psychic, one would think I'd know, but I'm blank on that one."

"I'm just … doing it."

Elmer says, "Leave Reggie alone. Stop being pests."

I watch as Elmer Mott slips into his own silly, boozy thoughts.

On most days, Reggie feels like he's molding a giant kingdom for some sandcastle contest. A grainy palace with towers, a terrace, a mote, a bridge. Reggie feels as though he's baking a very important cake. A pink, iced confection for a one-hundred and second birthday. He feels like he's tending to endless acres of crops that might save suffering starving children. A garden of corn, of tomatoes, of string beans, of carrots.

His truths and recipes are weighty now. When he was employed, Reggie owned responsibility. But now, jobless, crafting his recipes somehow feels important.

Reggie Lauderdale always slumbers in the blue room. Tonight, his bed scorches his skin. He is plagued by sweat, despite countless churning box fans. Dressed in only briefs, he stumbles down the hall in search of a thermostat. Reggie ventures into Dolly and Herb's suite. He switches on the cruel, stinging lights and his eyes instantly bulge in marvel. A vast collection of hand mirrors clog an entire wall. The space is crammed with candlesticks, vanities, jeweled lamps, records, glassy floors, a fur coat rumpled on a boat-like bed. Reggie wanders toward the closet. He unlatches the door and discovers shelves upon shelves of high-heeled shoes.

Reggie recalls his mother. Mrs. Lauderdale longed for heels and spent many long weekends slipping on each style. Once, she bought a marked-down heels and clicked around the house. The tick of her traipse sounded utterly smashing.

He'd said, "I can hear you everywhere, mommy."

"I feel like a starlet," she told him.

The following day his mother buried the heels in the bottom of a sidewalk trash can.

"When I'm trying to get some shut-eye, it all just feels so wrong." She'd explained, "And don't let your father find out, ok?"

Now, in a place quite unlike his home, Reggie stuffs his foot inside an unforgiving arch. He pushes and stomps and finally buckles in. Rising, he gains four inches. Reggie wobbles and wavers but soon begins to walk. And walk. And walk.

Reggie Lauderdale is trotting in a black pair of heels.

Click. Click. Click. Click. Click.

He hears the door moan behind him and flushes with fear.

Polly stands in the doorway, holding her crotch.

"Sorry," Reggie says and attempts to cover his bare body, "Sorry ... sorry. I was just playing around."

"I'm looking for the little girl's room. I have to pee so bad. I know it's the ninth door down, but I always lose count."

"Sure," is all that Reggie can say.

Polly giggles and tugs on her hair. "Look at *you*, Reggie," she delights.

"I'm just being a goof."

"You walk like a real pro. I've seen, like, thousands of girls in thousands of shows. They stink compared to you. And all you have on is undies. It's all you need. This should be your uniform."

"I'm just being silly."

"No. No. You look ... *beautiful*. You're a real sight."

"Don't tell Elmer. Okay?"

"Why not?"

Reggie grins.

"Keep walking. I'll try to hold my pee for this."

Reggie Lauderdale's face burns like a cinder. "You want me to walk?"

"Yes!" Polly smiles.

He struts. He vamps.

I see Polly clap.

She says, "You're such a looker."

Reggie feels as though he ornaments the whole wide world.

I feel this too.

※

In the kitchen, Elmer tips back a Long Island iced tea. He can feel tacky, dried up semen, tight on his torso. He starts scraping off his DNA. "I shoot, like, everywhere," he says and chuckles.

Beside him Doris sifts through Reggie's recipe cards. Elmer says, "Don't let Reg see you checkin' his stuff. He'll have a shit fit."

She shakes her head. "I think ... this is ... quite amazing."

"Reg and our neighbor are getting on real well. It's like the little brother program or whatever it's called. Weird. But I think it's good for him."

She continues poring through Reggie's recipes and does not respond.

Elmer says, "Reverend Rockwell might be a whack job. Who knows? Reggie likes him a lot, though."

Doris appears to be engulfed.

"You want a drink or something?' He nudges her. "Feel like jerking me off again?"

"This is ... perfect."

"Huh?" Elmer asks.

"Reggie's cookbook. It's ... basic, to the point. It's wonderful." She squints and her bulbous eyes shrink. "This should be *out there*. People *need* to read this."

Elmer sucks on a shard of ice. "Who knows?" he says, "Anything can happen. Talk to him about it."

Doris slaps her gown. "I'm talking to *you* about it."

"I know you're talking to me. I hear you, doll." Elmer pets her shoulder. He smells powder.

"Reggie is doing something special. When I first read his recipes, I thought ... wow, he's right. He's right about many, many things. We *should* be better. We *should* be good. We *should* take an interest in others. We *should* be kind and helpful. It's simple. Anyone can do it. And, Elmer, I've never truly done anything because I've never *had* to do anything. I've just been a wire hanger my whole life." She blinks. The only time Elmer has witnessed her do so. Her face begins to crinkle and her eyes gloss in sorrow.

He says, "Don't be sad."

"These recipes ... all of this ... it means something. I think it's important. This is something ... something you and Reggie could do together."

"What do you mean?"

"I'm saying that this is something you two could ... *provide* to people. Truth. Hope. You could really help people. And I'd like to help people too."

Elmer snuggles into her skeletal side.

Doris straightens, shrugs him away. "I'm thinking ... I'm thinking you two could be what Reverend Rockwell never was."

All Elmer can say is, "Um ..."

Doris blots away her tears, rises and begins to strut away. "You can both be bigger. You can be, like Reggie says, true. I have a psychic feeling about this."

Elmer says, "Is it that time of the month, doll?"

Recipe # 39

We need family. Mothers, fathers, sisters, brothers. They are all vital.

You can form your own family as well. Friends, cousins, neighbors, a mail carrier, the woman at the corner deli. There are so many special people around us. And they should be welcome in your clan. Anyone who makes you happy should be family.

Be sure to share how much you love them.

Everyone needs family. Especially you. Especially me.

Elmer Mott is stirred by whiffs of whiskey, perfume and hot buns. He awakes to a new day, and propping himself up, he sees Doris scribbling in a binder, tapping on a laptop.

Elmer digs sleep from his eyes. "Why are you up so early?"

"It's two in the afternoon." Doris replies. "I've been up since twelve."

"What are you doing, doll?"

She hits a button four times. "I'm, as they say, getting the ball rolling. Establishing a new form of divinity is extensive labor."

Elmer grimaces. "Huh?"

"I have so many visions. I can see it all."

"Hey … hey … it's too early for visions. Let's sleep." He collapses again and locks onto Doris' waif body.

She whispers, "I'm going to tell you what to do."

"I'll do whatever you want." He yawns. "After some sleep."

She pitches her pen and laughs, buries into Elmer's body. "We're going to change things."

"If you say so."

A flood of sunrays batter Reggie's burnt neck. At a neighborhood yard sale, he strolls beside Reverend Rockwell, eyeing vintage merchandise. Key chains, lunch boxes, hot plates, souvenir magnets. Reggie plucks up a dead alarm clock, whaps it twice and watches the hands start to tick. He continues searching. "Look," Reggie exclaims. "A copy of *Ana Karenina*. My mother read that book, like, a million times."

Reverend Rockwell says, "Big enough to be a door stop. Jesus. Say what you need to say and say it quick. Too many pages"

"That's why she liked it. It goes on and on."

"Not my taste, son."

Reggie clucks and looks skyward. "*Where* is Elmer?"

"Probably misbehavin' somewhere."

Reggie turns and sees Elmer scooping through a beat cardboard box. He asks Reverend Rockwell, "Have you read my cards yet?"

The man examines a filthy computer mouse. "I have," he replies. "And I have … no comments."

Reggie frowns. He feels himself deflate. His feels his insides cave. "Too silly? No good?"

Reverend Rockwell looks at Reggie. "They're practically perfect. Just keep going. And don't stop."

Reggie smiles and smiles.

Reverend Rockwell tells him, "You've got it, son. I wouldn't say so if I didn't believe it. Remember Recipe Number Eight. If you feel something, say it. I don't have to be your critic, your noise. I only have to encourage you. "The man snorts and sniffs.

Behind them, Elmer yells, "Hey! You guys!"

Reggie peers westward and sees Elmer gripping a bundle of plaid trousers. Red and yellow. Powder blue.

Elmer shouts, "They're all my size. Bonus!"

Reggie hollers, "You're going to look like an old man, Elmer!!!"

Recipe #44

You are beautiful. You are handsome. You are foxy. We all are.

You may not like your legs, but someone does. And why not? You may not like your hair, but someone does. And why not? You may not like your belly, but I do. The parts you despise may excite others.

And DON'T compare yourself to show business screens. Fiction! You were made this way for a reason. There is always a purpose.

So, celebrate your exterior. And everyone else's too. Tell Harriet she's a hot dame. Tell Roger he's striking. Tell yourself that you are gorgeous.

Reggie stomps his way toward the parlor, once again in only pumps and underwear. He enjoys his new stripped-down attire, far cooler now, and more at ease.

Elmer is eating creamed corn from a can. He asks, "You going naked these days? And you wear heels now too?"

Reggie smiles. "Yeah. I guess. It was sorta Polly's idea. But I like them."

Elmer smiles. "Yeah. Fuck it. If you want to, wear 'em."

"See, I like the sound they make."

"Tap, tap, tap." Elmer forks more kernels into his mouth. Two plop to the plush carpet.

Reggie laughs. "Have you seen my recipes? I can't find them."

"Uh, Doris was reading them. She thinks they're … what did she say … *massive*."

Reggie wrings with annoyance. "I didn't say she could look at them."

"Don't get pissy! She just grabbed them. But Reg, she says they're like, this new, amazing, thing. She made me read them. And I think so too." A belch punctuates Elmer's words.

Reggie's anger drips away.

"You're speaking up! You're saying shit – and not just stupid shit. Important shit. Most people don't have the nuts to say a single word."

He grins. "Thank you, Elmer."

"Doris wants to put them out there. She thinks it could help people. She says it's the coolest little cookbook ever."

Reggie files his pump across the floor.

Recipe # 77

You sleep. And, therefore, you dream. Maybe you don't remember all your dreams, but they do happen.

You also dream when not in slumber. You dream of becoming this. You dream of becoming that. You dream of doing such and such or so and so.

When you dream awake, it's easy to discard them.

But don't ignore your dreams.

They will save you, as they have saved me.

Recipe #82

You should throw your clocks and watches away. When you run your life by time, it creates bustle and distress.

Savor each second.

When you take the time to add up all your time, you'll discover you don't really have much time at all.

Right?

Between the dolls, Elmer is coiled within a mountain of messed linen. The afternoon sun fans his face. Elmer prods Polly's shoulder, but she is absent, astray in sleep.

Elmer snorts and tells Doris, "She's out."

Doris smoothes her hair and replies, "Polly has always been like this. When we were small, she'd fall asleep anywhere and everywhere. At fashion shows. In people's closets." Doris reaches over and snakes her hand inside his trousers. "Can we be inappropriate?"

Elmer cowers, covering his groin. "My dick is killing me. Like someone punched it again and again. You two got me using it too much."

"Don't be a child. Just give it a rest so you can use it later."

"Okay, doll," he says, cackling slyly. Since yesterday, Elmer's back has felt prickled and ablaze. "Can you scratch my back?" He asks.

"I suppose. If I must."

Elmer rolls onto his stomach and rests his head on his forearms. "Hard or soft?" She asks.

"Soft, I guess."

Doris sits on his rump and rakes her fingernails up and down his skin. She says, "You're an entertainer, Elmer. You're like a tomcat hipster. You're a host. And with Reggie, you'll create a stunning show."

"Reggie and I aren't what you think. We're just two guys that happen to be cousins, not some fucked up religious lounge act."

She pauses. "*I know*. I know. You're going to be *so* much more."

Elmer sighs with pleasure. "Harder, please."

"You look scruffy, by the way. You need a haircut."

"Hey, I like my hair. It's very ... *Elmer*."

Mel's Barber Shop clock has stalled at 11:11.

Elmer shifts in a leather chair, the cushion howling beneath him. Hair clippings carpet the floor. Stools are bandaged with black tape and each mirror is framed in business cards or children's school photos.

Elmer unfolds a day-old newspaper and scans the headlines. He reads, *The U.S. has Harsh Words for China*, and *America Won't Be Bullied!* Mel snips at a senior's hair. He says, "Don't know why you even want a haircut. Ain't got much to cut. Easiest eight-fifty I've made all week."

The customer laughs and mutters, "Old bastard."

Mel studies the man's head and seems satisfied. "Outta my chair, bucko." He chuckles, his gut swinging to and fro. He calls to Elmer, "Hey kid, what you in for?"

"Just a regular."

Mel levels his spear-like sideburns. "I think you need a hot shave too. Get your ass over here."

"Right-o."

Don Ho's "Tiny Bubbles" flits throughout the barbershop.

Cream glazes Elmer's collar and face. Three dollops stain his trousers. Elmer's head is slung back, a dotted cape buttoned around his neck.

Mel says, "Every fella needs a hot shave, you know."

Elmer doesn't reply.

"If you wanna be dapper. It's obvious."

"Whatever you say." Elmer feels the blade skim across his jaw. Prickles of delight scurry inside him. He thinks he might be lulled into a short and sudden nap.

Mel wipes his blade and asks, "So, what do you fashion yourself as? If somebody asked me to guess, I'd say you're a salesman. A rookie salesman."

Elmer is motionless, tranquil. "Nope," he says, "I'm not anything right now. Got no job. Got no ... what's that word ... occupation?"

"You've gotta be a something," Mel says. "Hey, some folks probably think about me and say, 'that old Mel ... he's just a fella who chops hair. Well, look out that window."

Elmer casts a glance toward the avenue and spots a silver luxury car boasting by the curb.

Mel continues, "That there is a fine, Cadillac. I dreamed of that baby. I wanted her ... for years and years and years ... and, now, I got her. She's mine. I call her Bet and she's all mine. Now, you and I can figure this out. What do you *really* do? It could be anything. A great lawn boy? A master coffee maker? A wonderful toilet bowl cleaner? It's all acceptable." Mel sweeps at stubble and foam.

Elmer clamps his eyelids. He says, "Well, I guess I'm a pretty funny guy. I think so, anyway. I'm a great cocktail mixer. And, you know, an alright person, generally."

Mel says, "All important occupations."

"I guess so."

"I know so, kid."

"Alrighty."

Elmer Mott gropes his buzzed scalp. His hair has never been so short. He tells himself, *I look clean*, and *I look … handsome*, and *I look … damn handsome*. He jogs into the bar room, craving seltzer.

With glittered legs, Doris spins and sips her cocktail. "Superb," she says. "No more mess." She smiles.

"Thanks, doll."

"You look grown up."

"That supposed to make me feel good?"

"You look your age," she says. "Oh … good news."

"What now?" Elmer asks.

She flicks her hand toward a stack of files. "The current recipes have all been … formatted for print. They're … stupendous."

Elmer lifts her drink and gulps. "So, you did it?"

Doris replies, "When I say I'm going to do something, I do it. And I did. Here it is." She clicks on a key and one of Reggie's recipes loads to life. #14. She says, "I'm industrious, no?"

Elmer guzzles more.

"Come over here. Please."

He scuffs closer.

"And bend down. Please."

He does as he's asked.

Doris strokes his head. "It's going to be a sensation," she says, tracing letters and shapes into Elmer's sun-baked scalp. "I can feel it. The psychic thing. *I know these things*. Plus, you're having a party."

"Huh?"

"A party. A reading. For the church and what-not. Reggie will recite a few recipes. You'll shake some hands. Everyone will drink and have a tremendous time."

Elmer says, "No way."

"Things have already been attended to."

"This is going to be a shit storm."

Earlier, Elmer was given a stack of party flyers. Before that, he'd ejaculated onto Polly's slick, slobbered face. An hour previous, he had fits, refusing to be "some freak religious guy." He then attempted to mix an El Presidente, but found no liquor.

Now, with bare feet and a naked pot belly, he shifts around on Reverend Rockwell's stoop. Elmer fingers the bell, once, twice, thrice.

The door opens and the sonic drifts of Marvin Gaye whisper out. A patchwork pussycat leers down the hallway and quickly gathers speed, preparing to launch for freedom.

Elmer asks himself, *Should I let him go or will he get lost?* and *Is he going to scratch the shit out of me?* and *Um ...?* He stops his reeling mind. Elmer dives for the floor, wrestling the feline into submission. The cat mews and purrs. "Asshole," Elmer says.

Reverend Rockwell is like a steeple above him, balancing a platter of white powder. "Thought someone was busting into the house. Why you manhandling Chowder?"

"Thought he might be a house cat. Didn't want him to escape and get eaten by wild things."

"Naw. He belongs to a fat lady down the street."

"Oh."

He chortles. "Thanks anyway, kid."

Elmer points to the dust. "What you got there?" He pulls on the cat's tail.

"Didn't want you boys to know ... but ... just some first-class cocaine."

Elmer chuckles. "How about offering some to your favorite neighbor?"

Ten minutes later I watch Elmer plug his nostril with a five-dollar bill. I see him inhale rows of illegal white dust. He snorts, sucks. Chokes a little. A synthetic drizzle oozes down his throat.

"It tastes good," Elmer exclaims. "It *feels* good."

Elmer is numb. Cinematic. Shined. Bulletproof. Wily. Clenched. Writhing on the inside.

Reverend Rockwell laughs.

Elmer says, "I feel like ... like the day's just started, but it's already two."

"The day *has* just started."
"Feels like it's gonna be a good one."

In a jittered spree, Elmer Mott finds bingo dobbers. He carefully makes a sign for the front lawn. *VOTE FOR ELMER MOTT: A NEW EL PRESIDENTE.*

CHAPTER EIGHT
MAYBE

RECIPE # 123

You can sleep in your house. You can eat in your house. You can sponge bathe in your house. You can take BMs in your house.

A house, though, isn't always a home. These two things are very different. One is a building and the other, a refuge. A home must be happy, safe and warm. Put people you love there. Put things you love there.

With effort, we can certainly erect a house, but if we're fortunate, we can also build a home.

RECIPE # 133

At any time, something amazing could happen. One never knows.

You may win the lottery or meet your lifetime love or become famous. You could save another from drowning. You could awake with the ability to soar the sky. You could receive a gift from a close friend.

There are countless possibilities. Consider them all! Maybe, if we believe these things might happen, well, maybe they will.

Please ... always believe in that special word.
Maybe.
Maybe.
MAYBE.

PARADE

RECIPE # 139

Outstanding telephone bills. Cankersores. A dented automobile. Constipation.

We are all plagued by troubles …

Yes, these matters deserve attention but don't let them rule you.

Remember: Celebration is the antidote. With joy, these situations will seem more manageable.

Have a tea party! Dance through the parlor! Have a sleepover! Eat gumdrops for dinner! Have a knock-knock joke contest.

Troubles are troubling.

And merriment is the cure!

Reggie Lauderdale feels like an attraction. He sits on the carpet, circled by bottles, recipe cards and a spare set of heels.

Doris tramps in, her sheer, ruffled gown in flight. She says, "I'll need all the new recipes by this afternoon. We need to wet people's appetite before the final printing."

Reggie gathers a bundle of cards. He jams them inside an empty bread bag and hands them over. "Here," he says, fringed with sighs. "Finished." He pinches his face.

Doris proclaims, "You seem … distressed."

"I just think … all this … could be a waste of time. I mean, who's going to care? Besides me. Besides you. Besides the Reverend."

She hikes up her couture and squats before him. "Last night, I re-read recipe ninety-nine and recipe thirty-eight. Recipe forty-two. And afterwards … I felt good." She is suddenly dressed in delight. "I felt … good. And I knew what to do, finally. I donated ten dollars to an animal shelter and I went to bed feeling … changed. Because of what you wrote. Reggie, you're doing incredibly well. Just breathe. Give it time. You will see."

Reggie hears a medley of clucking joy.

The door bursts open.

Elmer cradles a jumbo tin thermos.

Polly, flushed and winded, points a microphone toward Reggie. "It's lip sync contest time!"

"No. Not tonight," he says.

Elmer gut-chuckles. "Yes, cous. It is."

"*You'll* be a sensation." Polly says. "We'll all be a sensation."

Elmer begs, "Do it for me, Reggie? Please? Come on?"

Reggie snatches the thermos from Elmer's grasp. He gulps the mystery beverage and ignores the returning ache in his testicle. Reggie thinks, *Maybe I will sing.*

I watch the night churn forward.

Elmer Mott had gathered a bundle of party leaflets—belched—slipped on loafers—gargled with cola—revved the limo.

Now, at Mel's Barbershop, The Drifters' ballad "Sweets for my Sweet" twinkles above the humming clippers and whooshing hairdryers. A waiting senior sleeps. A toddler crunches on a pink lollipop.

Mel snips a panting patron. He tells him, "Be still, fella. I know you're nerved up, but relax. I'm gonna' chop your head off."

The customer fidgets in response. "*Oh.* No. Be careful. I'll be good. I'll be still." He is heaving, gripping the armrest.

Elmer shuffles over and holds out his flyer. "Can I put this somewhere? Please?" He asks.

Mel says, "Don't bother me now, sonny. Hair cutting is precise work."

"Oh. Yeah. Sorry." Elmer replies.

"Post whatever you like. Just pipe down."

"Sure."

Twenty minutes later, Elmer is sitting in a beat-up barber chair as Mel trims and tidies his neck.

Mel asks, "What's your advertisement for? Lost a puppy? Having a yard sale, or something?"

"No, just a party."

"Your tenth birthday?" He laughs.

Elmer sighs. "Um … no. Something like a church, but not *really* a church."

Mel fluffs his checked, yellow shirt. "Never thought you'd be god-fearing."

"I'm not. It's complicated. And why should I be afraid of some guy, especially some made up guy named Jesus Christ?"

Mel's trimmers boogey across Elmer's skin. Gooseflesh sprouts as he enjoys a new form of inner silence. Elmer asks, "Why do you think people say that? God-fearing?"

"Well," Mel says, "Way back when, we was all taught that God was everywhere to keep everyone in line. He was the boss. He was the head honcho. We were afraid of guys like him. So … they said, God-fearing."

Elmer considers Mel's reply. He thinks of Reverend Rockwell. He remembers St. Leo's Church.

I know these events remain stark in his memory.

He looks up at Mel, "In our church, there's no place for fear. We don't fear anyone. Nobody is a threat."

Elmer continues fastening flyers to storefronts, ATMs, trees, taxi windshields, Senior Center Bulletin Boards. He papers every inch of Jupiter.

"You can't be decoratin' town like you own it!" a sugared voice calls out.

Before him, Elmer sees a middle-aged black woman in athletic sneakers. "Hi," Elmer exclaims.

She sweeps the sidewalk. Tiny, meager mounds of litter mark her trail of cleanliness. "You can't just pin your papers everywhere."

Elmer scratches his groin, scuffing closer. "What if I promise to take 'em down next week? We have a deal?"

"Listen," she says, "I don't own this city either. I can't tell you what to do. But it just doesn't seem right."

Elmer leaps up and tacks a flyer to a 'SLOW' street sign.

"Motorists won't be reminded to drive *real* careful now," she says.

Elmer can taste her perfume, which chokes the air, stings his tongue. "Alright. Sorry." He jumps up and snatches it down.

"That's better," she says. "You a salesman?"

"No," he replies, amid laughter. "I just look like a salesman."

"You in advertising, then?"

"Sure. That sounds good. You a cleaning lady?"

She chuckles. "Somedays I am, I suppose." She motions to a huge building edged in greenery. "I work there. It's a sanctuary for the retired."

"An old folk's home?"

She shifts eastward. "That's a mighty rude way to say it, but yes."

"Well, that's what it is, right?"

"Sure. Yes. But you shouldn't be so … disrespectful. You should have manners." She begins sweeping again.

"Oh." Elmer is disarmed and fooled by his own brash words. He considers all the times he might have been cross or unkind. Such moments could have easily coasted by without him realizing. He asks himself, *Am I a jerk sometime*s" and *Do I act shitty*? Elmer tells the woman, "Sorry I'm such a fuck ass."

She dips her head toward the sidewalk and grins.

Elmer says, "I'm being serious."

"Fine."

"It's an apology."

"Job well done." She laughs again. "I'll forgive you if you hold my dust pan so I can get rid of this mess."

Elmer nabs the pan, crouches down and steadies himself beside her mounds of sand and litter.

"Someone has to clean these streets," she says. "If I don't do it, maybe no one will."

Elmer wants to tell her something special. Some weighty proclamation. But he doesn't know what to say. Finally, he blurts, "I think you're probably very, very nice. What's your name anyhow?"

She bats her dress down. "I'm Barb," she replies. "'Now, a little to the left. Get that pile over there."

Elmer obliges.

Barb says, "Sure. I suppose I'm nice." She sweeps some more.

A slight plume of dust washes over Elmer's face. "I think you're pretty, too."

Four of Elmer's flyers are hauled off by the wind.

Barb points. "Don't forget that pile by the post. Have to get that one."

Elmer scrambles to the pile. "Um … Barb? I'm trying to be a …"

"I know. You're trying to be a loverboy. I know."

"Oh. Okay." He peeps up at her.

"I'm thinking about it," she says.

"Well, that's something."

⁂

Reggie curses the heat. Epic warmth strikes Jupiter for yet another day.

He scowls at the soft, steaming asphalt, the fans, the weepy turf, the ocean's stink. He clutches a roll of paper towels and when sweat puddles in his armpits, he tears sheets off, dabs his skin and searches for a wastebasket.

Reggie peers out the window and spots a tennis court. Below, water spurts from a sprinkler, misting the grounds. He never knew that Dolly and Herb played tennis. He was certain they enjoyed horseshoes or cribbage, but not tennis. Reggie thinks, *Dolly has a tennis bracelet, maybe she needed a tennis court too.*

He asks Elmer to haul out kitchen stools. He asks Elmer to harness the sprinkler. He asks Elmer to mix a bubblebath.

Now, beside the net, Reggie is sloth-like. A slight shower of droplets dot his flesh. A refreshment is locked between his thighs. He exclaims, "It's hotter than hell out here. Do you think hell is hotter than this?"

"How can I smoke if I'm getting rained on?" Elmer asks.

"You'll be fine for five minutes. Jesus." A massive bird sails through the air above, circling, cawing,. Reggie says, "Look. A bald eagle, I think."

Elmer squints and looks up. "No," he says. "They don't come round here. That's just a hawk. A bald eagle is bigger. And longer."

"Don't know why they're our country's symbol. They look downright ... *mean*."

Elmer shrugs.

"I'd rather it be a bunny rabbit or a duckling. They're much nicer."

"You want some wimpy animal representing America? The eagle? He's all power and class."

"I'm just saying he looks a bit ... devilish."

"He looks awesome. Fuck it." Elmer groans. "I'm sweating my nut sack off. I gotta get a shave and Doris asked me to go into town."

Reggie opens his mouth to catch the rain. He reaches over and touches Elmer's cheek. His cousin feels stubbly, scruffy. "I'm worried," Reggie finally says.

"Why now?"

Reggie fiddles with his bracelet. "This whole cookbook, recipe, church thing. It's a big production."

"Don't be dramatic."

"I'm just writing this stuff for fun. And you and I, we should be invisible. We shouldn't exist."

Elmer clasps his unbuttoned trousers.

Reggie is pricked with nuisance. "Nothing makes any f'ing sense, Elmer."

"Calm down. Jesus Christ."

Reggie's flesh feels chilled, but as soon as the spinning spout clucks away, he burns again.

I know he is trying to ram down this newness.

The mansion.

The recipes.

Reverend Rockwell.

Truths.

Purpose.
Direction
The Dolls.
The future.
The heat.
The heels.
Drink.
I know that Reggie Lauderdale is tail-spinning.

Elmer pinches out only cashews. He concludes that medleys should not be displayed. Peanuts. Walnuts. Even Maharanis. They all deserve their own decorative dish. *What if someone doesn't like that nut?* He sorts them all, his fingertips greased and glued with salt rocks.

Polly winds down the staircase, decked in a sheer pink gown. "Oohh," She stutters among coughs. "Nuts. You've already *gone* nuts, Elmer."

"Obviously," he replies.

"I like you being nuts." Polly hops from the final step. "Are we gonna fuck soon?"

Elmer grouses, "Naw …"

"You never say no, Elmer."

"What … *are* we? You and me and your sister? What do we … *mean?*"

Polly swishes toward Elmer. She cranes down and scoops a handful of pistachios.

"I mean, what am I to you?" He asks.

"Try not to think too hard, Elmer. You're asking tricky questions," Polly replies.,

He pushes the nuts aside, licks his fingers and lights a cigarette.

Polly sits beside Elmer, smoothing hser bangs. "What's the matter?"

Elmer exhales a surge of smoke. "Are we boyfriend … and girlfriend … and girlfriend?"

Polly nods, lips puckered. "You like us and we like you. It's not eighth grade stuff. There's no fucking homecoming dance."

Elmer taps his cigarette above a pony glass. Embers hiss in the abandoned malt. "I don't know. I always thought I'd have a lady to ... you know, *be* my lady."

"You've got *two* ladies, Elmer."

"But, what if ... what if I decide I want another lady?"

"You want three?" Polly practically shrieks.,

"I mean just one. But someone else. Someone without a sister?"

Polly pitches a nut across the room. "You know, you don't talk to girls too well."

"Sorry." Elmer's neck becomes slack. His head drops to the carpet.

Polly says, "So, you've got a crush or something?"

"I guess so."

"This girl ... this girl without a sister ... could she be good for you?"

"I think so ... I think she could."

Before, Elmer heard Reverend Rockwell holler over the fence. He wobbled, sleepy, to his neighbor's estate. Minutes ago, they both inhaled two long lines of cocaine. Right now, Elmer and Reverend Rockwell are perched in the canary-colored kitchenette, engrossed in a hand of rummy.

Elmer, sopped in sweat, gathers two pair of kings. Sevens too.

Reverend Rockwell exclaims, "Damn, son. I think you're bootin' my ass."

Elmer chuckles, cocksure.

I know that Elmer feels like he's on vacation. An adventure won from a mustard company sweepstakes. I know he has always wondered if people actually win such contests. In this case, Elmer has won big-time.

"Coke is fun, Reverend," He declares.

Eclipsed by drugs, Elmer is supreme and sunny. Atwinkle with gritted smiles.

"Cocaine *is* entertaining," Reverend Rockwell agrees.

"Can't wait for party night."

"Me too. Doris asked me to welcome folks at the door and keep the roughnecks out."

Elmer sighs like an imploding gasket. "She's a piece of work sometimes. Mouthy. Bossy."

"Indeed. Still, Doris has really pulled everything together. It'll be fun. Fun, fun, fun. And special."

"I'm going to get hammered."

Reverend Rockwell laughs. "No doubt there."

"Could I get some snowy stuff for the party?"

Reverend Rockwell drops a foursome of jacks onto the tabletop. "We should get a bit for everyone, no? You'd have to be my helper, though."

"I can add that to my resume." Elmer folds his hand of cards. "Every occupation is important."

Elmer Mott is jaw-clamped, his gums gleaming. He can smell the fry-battered landscapes inside the kitchen as he fighsts off nausea. He sees Doris who towers before the stove, pulling on a cigarette.

Doris says, "I knew you'd be home about now. Psychic stuff. I concocted a casserole. It's all I know how to cook. My mother made them every night when we weren't in Paris or Milan. You can put anything in it. My dad always flushed them down the toilet. Plumbers were called. What not. Oh well."

Elmer hoists himself onto the countertop. "I already ate at the Reverend's. Sorry."

She peers into the golden dish. "Wish my fantastic, psychic brain knew that too."

"I'll have some for a snack. Or breakfast. Just don't be mad at me."

Doris flits toward the refrigerator and yanks an uncorked bottle of champagne out. "My role isn't a … housewife, Elmer. I'm not *that* girl."

Elmer pulls down a string of Christmas garland from a cabinet knob. He drapes it around his neck.

She says, "I hope you're ready for the party."

"Sure as shit."

"Polly will help Reggie. I'll decorate. You do the drinks. Everything should be … stupendous, if everyone does what I say. It will be *stupendous*."

"What if folks don't show?"

"They'll show. We're doing something. A good thing."

"I guess."

"Invite your new girlfriend, maybe(if you want)."

Elmer guffaws and drums his forehead. "Is that okay?."

"Perfectly fine. I'm never going to be your first lady."

"Good, I guess."

Reverend Rockwell coasts into the Pilot's Diner.

Elmer says, "Hey … I know this place. Good food."

"Ready to be Santa's little helper? Keep still. Be quiet. This is just a pick-up."

"Got it, captain."

Elmer Mott smells meat loaf. "Wanna get an ice cream soda?" He asks the Reverend.

"Not hungry, son," Reverend Rockwell replies. "Maybe a coffee, though."

Laurie Fooz swanks from the kitchen, knits her mouth and whips her head sideways.

Elmer grins. "Hi, there," he says.

Laurie swishes. "Well, Christ. Never thought I'd catch sight of you again." She wears dark lips and fringed black gloves. Her tassels swing wildly. "How have you been?"

"Super."

"Back for a Number Ten Special? A Number Five?"

Reverend Rockwell coughs. "We're just meeting some friends."

Laurie Fooz stands like a storefront mannequin. "I see." She laughs.

Elmer is buzzed with nerves. He fumbles in his front pocket. Lighter. Coins. Linty sucker. Mangled party flyer. He yanks the flyer out and smiles at Laurie. "Got something for you."

RECIPE # 144

When we were children, adults would ask, "What do you want to be when you grow up?" We told them, "A prince train conductor." We told them, "A ladybug." We told them, "A cowgirl lifeguard." We told them, "A dragon."

Everything was possible.

Now, of course, we are grown. We have bills, and babies, and chores. Each chance has shriveled. So we say things like, "I wish I could be a dental hygienist."

Do not let this happen. Take back the right to be whatever you want. A flower. A crooner. A farmer. A princess. A president. A bumblebee.

Today, I'm going to be a pop idol.

What will you be?

Come on ... tell me.

Elmer stretches across the sofa, shirtless. Clumps of dried deodorant cling to his underarm hair.

"Time to get up," Doris says, tramping in.

"I'm sleepy, doll. I need a little catnap."

She drops a cream-colored book onto his chest.

"Book club or something?" He asks.

"Hardly," she says, her She replies, hands welded to her hips. "It's Reggie's cookbook. It's finished. And all the copies are here. Thousands."

Elmer thumbs through the paperback. He smiles. "Fucking perfect. Reg must be so happy."

"He didn't want to give it a glance. Said it made him too nervous."

"Typical."

He turns to the second page and reads his cousin's dedication: *To Elmer Mott, thank you for saving me. I love you.*

"It's time to go." Doris proclaims.

"Go where?"

"Anywhere, Elmer. We gotta give 'em away. All of them. It's time." Doris smiles, majestically.

"So, no nap, huh?"

Elmer tears toward Mel's Barber Shop.
Elmer arrives at the retirement home.
Elmer hotfoots to the corner candy store.
Elmer tears toward the senior center.
Elmer arrives at the local comic book joint.
Elmer hotfoots to Sal and Betty's Market.
Elmer tears toward the miniature golf range.
Elmer arrives at the almost abandoned strip mall.
Elmer hotfoots to the local pub.

Hey Barb,

It's me, Elmer. The guy who helped you sweep the sidewalk. I hope you're doing great. Here's an invitation I've been covering the town with, just for you. Sorry about that. Anyhow, it's just me and my cousin and some friends. We're gonna have fun! And I would love it if you could come. It would mean a lot. See you there. I hope.

Sincerely,

Elmer

CHAPTER NINE
RAPTURE

Reggie Lauderdale twirls his pen like a baton. He sits, rooted on the rear turf, waiting for more recipes to pedal forward. *The Cookbook, Volume Two*.

More, more.

Someone asks, "You live here, fella?"

He grinds his heels into the grass and spots a girl he thinks is about eight or nine years old. Her wheat-colored skin is sopping and her pigtails are past frayed. She strains with a picnic basket.

"You the owner?" She asks.

"Sure. Why? Who are you?"

"I'm an entrepreneur. Selling cups of punch for a dollar."

Reggie smirks. "From a basket?"

"Yep. Too young for a license, so it ain't like I can drive no van around."

"Then you're a traveling entrepreneur?"

"Why do you have them pumps on?" she asks. "Aint you a man?"

Reggie's face rumples. He grins. "None of that matters. Boys can wear what *they* want and girls can wear what *they* want. You're probably too young for any of this anyhow."

"Shoot. Don't be like that, fella. I like to wear baseball caps and cleats and, sure, my mommy don't like it, but ... I do it anyways." The little girl drops her picnic basket.

Reggie smiles, "Alright ... fine. Maybe you're *not* too young. Tell me your name."

"I'm Nell," s" She replies. "I own Nell, Incorporated."

Reggie rips blades of grass from the earth and tosses them into the air, wistfully, carelessly. He feels Nell's age. "So, Nell. Can I buy a cup of punch?"

"Surely. Would you like your punch plain or fancy?"

"What's the difference?"

"Plain is just plain fruit punch. Fancy is punch with a few drops of moonshine."

"Make mine *extra* fancy, please" Reggie says.

Nell asks, "Them pumps hurt your toes?"

"Sometimes" he says, smiling. "But they don't look half bad. So, why do you prefer cleats, Nell?"

She pours the elixir into a dinky, paper cup. "Well, cleats dig into the ground. They help you run. And be fast and strong. I gotta be both *real* fast and *real* strong, Mister."

"Sounds perfect."

Nell hands Reggie his beverage. She says, "I keep my cleats in the dresser drawer. Mama threatened to toss 'em in the garbage. When nobody's home, I put 'em on and race all around the yard." She is smiling and smiling.

"How do you … feel when you wear them?"

"I feel … real good … happy, I guess. Sounds dumb, right? They're just cleats."

"Sounds like your cleats are special."

Nell shrugs. "I dunno."

Reggie Lauderdale says, "My heels make me feel good too. And, like, strong. cleats So, I imagine our shoes are kinda the same."

Nell simpers. "We're like twins. Shoe twins. The kid kind and the grown-up kind."

"Sure, twins."

Reggie asked Nell to indulge in a break. His face had soured after drinking her fancy punch. He had asked if he could touch her hair and now, he can see her pop socks and smell the maple syrup still slick on her lips. Reggie asks, "How did you get into running your own corporation?"

"It's just something I thought up. And I like working for only me."

"Makes sense."

"Better than being a, I don't know, mama or a mail lady."

"Well, it looks like you're doing a good job ... *at your job.*"

Nell motions to the spattering of cards, creased notes and pens. "What's all that?"

"I'm just writing a book," ' he says. "Well, another book, I guess."

Nell wrenches a clump of cash from her picnic basket and begins to flatten and smooth the notes. "You're a real-life writer?"

Reggie sips his beverage. Punch trickles on his leg and he wipes it away.

Nell unfolds a five-dollar bill. "Let me hear some of this book then. Go on, read it."

"It'll bore you, probably."

Nell says, "You don't have to be shy. And I'll tell you what I think. Promise."

Reggie sifts through the blanket of cards. Recipe Number Twenty B, Recipe Number Nine B, Recipe Number Thirty-Three B, Recipe Number Eight B. Eventually, he settles on Number Nineteen B. Reggie tilts his head eastward. "Recipe Number Nineteen B. Hey, you're smart. I'm smart too. Sure, we all don't know how to do long division and sure, we all don't know the capital of Delaware. But you and I are certainly smart at something. Maybe you know about stamps or presidents or painting. Maybe you know about birds or cross-stitching or dishwashing. Everyone has their strengths. We are all brilliant at something. It cannot be measured or defined. Sure, what's-his-name has a big degree, but he still knows nothing about making freeze box cookies. So ... you're smart. And I am too. We're all smarty-pants, you know." Reggie drops the card in the grass and sighs. "I'm still working on that one," he says.

Nell stuffs the money inside her basket. "Hmmmm. Makes you think about stuff. My baby brother always tells me I'm not smart. Calls me a dummy and a stupid head."

Reggie grazes her hand. "You're not a dummy *or* a stupid

head. You're brilliant. You're a businesswoman. I would never have thought to sell fancy punch. But you did. And you're doing what you want."

Nell smiles, "Maybe so. Well, thanks. I feel smarter now that you say so."

Reggie smiles and asks, "Do you like parties, Nell?"

⁂

Reggie squeezes his recipe cards. He waits on Reverend Rockwell's sofa, trying to watch a cable cooking show. The host is round with dark, coiled hair. Her name is Connie. She dices peppers. Cuts cubes of butter. Reggie has been waiting for the Reverend for almost twenty minutes. He is in the bathroom in the midst of what he fondly calls "a meeting." Even with the door closed, Reggie can hear the overhead fan clunk, burp and chug. Connie salts slick chicken breasts. Reggie calls out, "Hurry, Reverend! I don't want to be laaaate. It's our party!"

"You can't rush these sorts of meetings, son!" He hollers. "I gotta do my business too."

Reggie rises and stamps over to the bathroom. He smells a horrid stench. Onions or garlic or rotten deviled eggs. "I really, really need your help."

"You dying?"

"Well, no, 'course not, but ..."

"Then give me some peace, please."

Reggie begins shifting, his heels aclick. "I'm nervous about the party and I can't find the right recipe to read. I don't want to look like a moron."

Reverend Rockwell grunts. "Reggie, you've You've learned how to *be* ... you. You can do the unbelievable, but only if you believe. I need you to believe."

Reggie hears a splashy plop. "I'll try."

"Now ... get going. See you at the siesta. Or fiesta. Whatever the Spanish call party."

"Okay."

Elmer Mott snorted a trail of cocaine—shaved his pubic hair too short—swilled a shot of whiskey—applied expired cologne—choked down a hunk of cheese—drenched his hair in the sink. He now attempts to iron a pair of plaid trousers. The cream and yellow stripes refuse to uncrimp. "Cock biter!" he shouts.

Doris breezes in. "The absurdity."

Polly trails behind. "Let me do that." She wrestles the iron from Elmer's clench.

"I can do it."

"Just relax. Stop being a psycho!"

Doris passes Elmer a card. "Here's your speech. I wrote it today. It's just a simple greeting. I borrowed a sound system from a DJ my dad fucked and they're installing it now. He also offered some strange lighting ... who knows if it works. I'm indifferent at this juncture." Doris adjusts her sleeve of bracelets.

Polly says, "Jesus fucking Christ ... everyone just calm down." A storm of steam gushes around her. "This is a party. We're supposed to have fun and ... get messy."

"This is a vital event, dear sister," Doris replies.

"I know. But ... *now* ... let's just enjoy it." More steam billows, slanting across her smile. "I mean, what the fucking fuck, people. I thought we were doing this to *live*. But this party is already making me wanna die."

Elmer adjusts his boxer shorts and sighs. "Let's just *relax*." He turns to Doris, clenching her waist. "Polly's right. Let's live. But, I have to say ... Doris, you're amazing. I'm so happy that you did all this. That you ... helped with Reggie's ideas. I think you could rule the world if you wanted to."

Doris grins. Her eyes shutter thrice. "Thank you, Elmer. You know, I'm just taken by you ... and Reggie as well."

Polly snorts. She rips the iron's cord from the socket. A tiny spark flutters. "Yeah, yeah," she says, "love, love, love. Let's go!"

Doris claps, grandly.

Polly screams.

"Fuck yeah!" Elmer whoops.

Elmer slowly pads into the room. He sees his cousin sitting on the bed, pristine. Spangled pumps and perfectly cropped curls and glossy thighs and recipe cards.

Reggie is breathing hard.

Elmer says, "If your dad could see you now …"

Reggie cocks his head. "My stomach hurts so be quiet, please." He bows toward the carpet.

"Let's not have an episode. It's just a little get together. And hey, I'll be next to you all night. If you get too nerved up, I'll burp ten times."

"Don't do that."

"I could fart too."

"No!" Reggie smiles.

"I could show everyone my dick and balls."

Reggie chuckles.

Polly whisks in, her locks cruising, dancing through the air. She hurries to Reggie and drapes a sparkled sheet around his neck. "I've decided it's all about fucking capes." Polly says, "And since you're without shirt … or pants … it'll keep you warm."

Elmer says, "He looks gay enough already. Don't you think? Heels and briefs?"

"Shut up. It's super. And for you, I made this." Polly hands him a lime checked shirt. "It's to match your pants and old man hat."

"Thanks, doll."

Polly huffs, "You both owe me a very, *very* large cocktail." She ticks away.

Elmer retrieves a vile from his pant pocket. "Here," he says, "Sniff some."

"We're doing drugs now? This is a nightmare. Where did you get that?"

"It's a secret."

"Don't be difficult."

"The Reverend."

"He's a drug dealer?" Reggie asks.

"Well, I guess you could say he's a drug dealer, yes, but only a bit of a drug dealer."

"He surprises me every day. Is this going to kill me, or make me go nutty?"

"I don't think so. Just do it." Elmer slides his shirt on. "The curtain's about to rise, cous."

※

Reggie Lauderdale is poised at the vanity, reading his recipes over and over again.

He hears disco claps and alien chatter and guffawing and clinking tumblers.

Reggie weaves his hands together. "Dear God," he prays, "I know we haven't spoken for a while … not since all the … *mess you made*. There's a huge part of me that hates you. But I can't be negative now. There is no time and no energy. *You* have to make this party, this cookbook, this … new world … a sensation. I am not asking. I am … demanding. You owe me.

The door whines open. andElmer smiles. "It's time."

Reggie barely utters, "I know."

※

Elmer tells his cousin, "We're going to be amazing." His legs wobble as they reach the top of the staircase.

Reggie says, "There are so many people."

"I know! Crazy!"

I watch the followers mingle downstairs. I watch them smoke cigars, chug screwdrivers. I see a cafeteria worker and a billionaire and a grandfather and an actress.

Doris tells Elmer, "Just strut, wave, and of course, *smile*."

"I'll do my best," Elmer says.

Music bumps and bounces, swelling in volume.

Elmer tugs on Reggie and they both descend. He remembers

to wave, even offers a thumbs up. And in no time at all he is chilled by applause and whoops and hollers and hoots.

Confetti storms like a ticker tape parade.

"Thanks for coming!" Elmer shouts.

I watch a postal worker jig in place. I watch a former pageant girl twirl in endless circles.

Elmer and Reggie reach the final step.

A man with a casted arm passes Elmer a microphone.

Reggie tells him, "Good luck."

"None needed."

Squelching sounds bark from the speaker box. Elmer sighs into the microphone. He gropes for his speech, finally finds it, and sighs once more.

"Elmer for president!" someone yells.

"Welcome. Everyone. To our party. And thank you for reading Reggie's Cookbook. So ... some call us a church, but we're really not. We're just cousins. Cousins with ideas and thoughts. But someone close urged us to share them. So, that's what we're doing. We don't care if you're a Christian, a firefighter, a Jew, a trans girl, a Buddhist, a porn star. Here, with this book of recipes, everyone should feel at home."

The partygoers clap and cheer. Someone shoots a water gun.

"So please make yourselves comfortable and have a *terrific* time."

The crowd cheers louder still still.

"I'd like to introduce the author of our *Cookbook*, Mr. Reggie Lauderdale!"

Peals of angst streak through Reggie but he pouts, waves, winks, begins to read. He says, "Recipe number sixty-seven. We all need beliefs. Maybe you believe in Santa. Maybe you believe in fate. Maybe you believe in macaroni and cheese. I don't know. But I beg you ... if you believe in something, whatever it is ... please *believe* in it. And believe in yourself ... believe in your loved ones ... every day and all day long. I also ask that you believe in something larger. *I* believe that someone is out there and he or she is watching and listening and caring." Reggie chuckles. "I don't know everything. But I know that I believe in all of you. So, please believe in me too. And believe in these words."

Reggie hears a glass shatter on the floor.

Elmer nabs the microphone, "Come on people. Let's have some applause."

Howls and clapping hands shower the room.

"I love you!" a woman shouts.

"I love you too," Reggie says and he reads more and more recipes to his followers.

Drunk with pride, Elmer cuts through the crowd, searching for Barb. Golden dance hall lights bore over him. He shakes many, many moist hands.

"Did ya really think I'd show up?"

Elmer turns to see Laurie Fooz, wearing a pants suit. A bandana too. She poses like a centerfold.

"Well, I came," she says.

Elmer instantly beams, falling into Laurie Fooz. "I'm so happy you're here," he says. "Reggie is … somewhere?"

"This is truly fucking fantastic. Your mother would be proud … if she were like me."

Elmer takes both her hands, cackling.

Reggie finishes his bubblebath. He is basking in grand finery like the Hollywood idols his mother celebrated.

I can feel the rapture in him.

Suddenly, Polly pulls his hand, steering him through the flock of followers.

"Where is Elmer?" he asks.

Polly replies, "Mingling. You know, kissing babies and signing tits."

"Can we sit?" Reggie asks. "I need to just … sit."

"Let's go left," Polly says.

Techno zips and bleeps romp through the mansion. A woman wearing an eye patch pinches Reggie's nipple.

Polly laughs.

"Wait, wait!" Reggie says. ~~Hwhen~~ he sees a young man collapsed in the corner. The man is weeping, openly. Overgrown tresses trickle down his neckline. Reggie asks, "Are you alright?"

"I'm good," the boy says and sniffles. "I'm great, really."

"Are you on drugs?" Reggie asks. "Why are you crying?"

"I just feel so good here. Recipe Number Sixty-Six and Recipe One-Hundred and Four really got to me. I'm trying to do good. And it feels ... *good*."

Reggie is spooked. He attempts to conjure a perfect reply, but can only say, "In that case ... I say, have a drink. And rejoice in *being good*."

Polly says, "Being the priest is a big job, huh?" She snorts

Reggie Lauderdale autographs the boy's leg, tosses a kiss to a trio of seniors and stamps away in search of a private couch.

A film of smoke blanches the sparse room.

Elmer sees half-swilled drinks and used condoms and crammed ashtrays and crumpled flyers and a solitary stray loafer. "Fuckin' trash," he says.

Someone flicks his shoulder. Doris.

"In the future I'm planning to pass a trash bag around."

"Oh, yeah. This place is a dump."

"For donations, not trash. Events like this cost money."

"Again? Really, doll?"

She exhales loudly. "All these people think you're ... *really* something. And I'm certain that next time, countless more will come."

"Don't get out of control. Who is gonna to clean this mess up? I can feel a hangover coming on."

"I paid a Girl Scout troupe to come over." She replies, "I said we'd buy a bunch of their cookies and wafers. I'll make sure they do a good job." Doris whips away.

I know that Elmer is awhirl, speeding high and super drunk. But soon he thinks, *Barb didn't come. She's not here. Barb didn't come.*

Reggie ticks out to the abandoned patio. An airplane winks across the skyline.

Someone says, "Mister?"

Nell. She is carrying her picnic basket, her braids severely savage.

Reggie says, "Nell … you made it, but … shouldn't you be in bed?"

"What a doggone great party! Nell replies. "Never done so much jitterbuggin' in all my life."

Reggie's mouth sweeps into a smile. "That makes me happy, Nell."

"I made a whole lot of new customers tonight. And they all wanted fancy punch. I ran out of moonshine! I'm about rich!"

Reggie glances down and sees that Nell is wearing her cleats.

"What do ya think?" She taps the pavement.

"Very nice. Sporty."

"Thanks." Nell smiles. "I like yours too. Hey, Mister, is it okay if I stop by tomorrow and run around for a bit?"

"Of course," Reggie replies.

Elmer narrows his blurred vision, steadying himself, wall to wall. He spots a drowsy blonde girl. A middle-aged, sweater clad man bouncing on a sofa.

Elmer sways on, calling, "Reg? Reggie?"

Reggie Lauderdale is dancing with Laurie Fooz. They shimmy and jerk and snag.

Laurie says, "Never knew you boys were *arch bishops* ... or whatever they're called!"

Reggie laughs, his mouth agape. Gleefully, he dances on.

"Reggie!"

Glossed in sweat, Elmer heaves before him.

"What?!" Reggie says.

"Let's go. Let's go." He is staggering.

Laurie slinks up to Elmer and tugs on his shirt collar. "Dance with us!"

"I'd love to, but not now, gorgeous. I need a minute with Reg."

Laurie flaps her hands and swings away.

Reggie says, "Are you having a crisis or something?"

He knuckles his left eye. "Let's just ... talk for a while. I'll feel better if we talk for a while."

Reggie sits with his cousin on the red room's bed.

Elmer's head plummets to Reggie's lap. "I just need to calm down."

"You can't do so much of that powder stuff. I'm pretty sure it's poison."

Elmer hacks.

Reggie does as his mother would when he was ill from flu or frightened of TV killers. He rubs Elmer's head, traces faint shapes into his buzz cut. He scrawls the word, *yes*, and *no*, and *Friday*.

"Did you have fun?" Elmer asks.

"I did. It was like ... I don't know ... nothing else. And you did great."

"Thanks, Reg. I'm just so ... fucking sad. I invited Barb ... and she didn't come. She doesn't like me. She doesn't care about me. Women ..."

"Everything will be okay."

Elmer struggles to belch. "Hey, do you remember home? Maria? Mrs. Lolly? The arcade?"

"I do. Our lives are so ... different now, huh?"

"Keep rubbing. Don't stop. Can you read some recipes to me?"

Reggie fingers the waistband of his briefs and plucks out some cards. "Any requests?"

"No. I love them all."

Reggie continues to caress Elmer's head. He is sure the recipes will cure his cousin's sickness. He reads, "Recipe Number Ninety-Four ... Just take a breath ..."

CHAPTER TEN
SHOESTRING CARNIVAL

Thirty suns have scaled the sky.

For Reggie Lauderdale and Elmer Mott, growth is brimming. New smiles. New laughter. I watch as they mix countless cocktails, dance barefoot and scribble more autographs.

I see the dolls glide like couture ghosts. I see Laurie Fooz chatter amid lungful's of cigarette smoke. I see Nell profit from the sale of her fancy drinks. I see Reverend Rockwell applaud the spin of another funk anthem.

This shoestring carnival flares for days on end. Recipes and truths are the hub of their happiness. I delight in watching them all feel *good*.

Three more parties pass.

Vodka.

Handshakes.

Ash.

Someone wearing a motorbike helmet.

Sopping coasters.

A new recipe.

Gin.

More dance anthems

Vermouth.

Hope.

Someone wearing a ski mask.

Joy.

Another muddied floor.

Lubricants.

One stray pill.

Truth.

Elmer herds the limousine down Jupiter's shoreline, searching for Barb's retirement home. Soulful songs quietly pluck and tweak. Elmer mashes his cigarette. He speeds by a mangled pup and finally sees the house. *Her* house.

After snorting a line of cocaine, he raps on the door.

A shrunken, female senior appears, topless. "Good afternoon. You Marty?" she asks.

"Uh … no." Elmer avoids staring at her nakedness. "Hello, Miss. I'm looking for a lady named Barb."

The woman yells, "Hey, Barb. There's some tomcat out here for ya!"

Barb emerges carrying a roll of paper towels. She ushers the woman sideways, "You can't forget to wear a shirt, Mildred. You've got to remember these things. Very important." She turns to Elmer. "Back again, huh?"

"I guess I am."

"Well, how are you?"

"I hate when people say, 'good,' or 'great', even when they're not. I'm sort of in the middle." He fiddles with old receipts inside his pant pocket. "I guess you must have lost your invite to my real big and important party."

"Oh. No. Had a full moon sort of night. Ms. Wethering had the flu and Mr. Kazdan was back to his old self. Tossin' chairs and lamps."

"I was looking for you.' Elmer mumbles. "I was waiting for you."

Barb scoots closer and rakes her hands through Elmer's wet locks. "Must not be used to this heat yet," she says. "You're nothing, but soggy."

Elmer shrugs, "Yeah. Oops." He he steps back.

Barb tears two sheets of towels free and gingerly dabs at Elmer's skin.

He feels a slight, sweet sensation.

"You look a mess," she says.

"Why didn't you come see me?"

"I told you. I couldn't."

Elmer clucks. "I know you probably say stuff like, 'I don't *need* no man to make *my* life …'"

"I sure *don't* go around town saying such ridiculous things. I know what kind of woman I am. And so do you."

"What? Do women want a parade?"

Barb laughs, open-mouthed. She gently dries Elmer's cheeks, Elmer's chin, Elmer's forehead.

He asks, "If you won't come see me … can I come see you?"

"Okay. Okay. It's the senior center's ziti supper next Wednesday. Have to bring my folks along. And I've got someone special I'd like you to meet. His name is Clancy. You can help him for a bit and then we'll have a proper meal."

"Alright, then," Elmer says, smirking.

RECIPE #77B

There is no reason we can't practice hope. Without hope … optimism … our days will not be bright. There will only be darkness.

Hope for sun. Hope for re-runs of your favorite television program. Hope for candor. Hope for liveliness. Hope for friendship. Hope for comedy. Hope for the almost perfect Wednesday. Hope for pizza. Hope for absolute love.

Hope and hope and hope.

When you believe you have nothing at all, there's always hope.

I know this.

Once again Reggie Lauderdale searches for Dolly's tennis bracelet. The bar, the rooms, the beds, the pantry, the pool. This occurs daily. One moment it gleams and twinkles on his wrist, yet hours later it turns truant. He knows that booze-filled nights do not give birth to clear minds and memories. Opening the front door, Reggie peers down the walkway.

"Hello? Hello?"

Reggie hears an unknown voice. Is it coming from the mansion next door? Or is it merely in his still-drunk mind?

"Hello? Hello?"

Reggie finally replies, "What?"

A trio of muscled boys emerge from the side yard. Each sports glassy, slicked hair, above denim shorts and tight undershirts. To Reggie, they look identical.

"Can I help you?" Reggie asks.

One boy says, "We're lookin' for Reggie or Elmer, or Reverend Rockwell or the dolls."

Reggie says, "I'm Reggie. Are you the religious kind asking for cash?" He struts nearer, clicking across the cobble.

Another boy says, "I guess we're becoming sort of religious, but we don't want any money from you. We slept on your lawn last night. Drove all the way from Malibu."

"Why?"

"Well, we want to be part of your church. A friend of a friend told us about it. The parties. The recipes. We think ... *I think* ... we should be doing something better."

Reggie's head see saws.

The most hulking boy says, "Your cookbook is really fucking great. I think my favorite is number forty-five. Or thirteen. Anyhow, we want to join your church. If you'll have us?"

Reggie's gives a charmed-filled pose. "Well, what are your qualifications? What are your credentials? What did you do in Malibu?"

The first boy replies, "We were models. Actors, really ... porn actors."

"I see."

"We still do it ... but only for the money ... we came to start afresh ... you know, like you. And ... can we use your bathroom?"

Reggie grins. "Of course. And grab yourself a snack in the kitchen if you can find one."

Reggie watches Christmas bulbs bob in the pool. Giddy from drugs, he fumbles for his cocktail. He fishes ice cubes from his glass and pitches them at Nell, Laurie Fooz and the dolls. "Cool down time!"

"Enough," Doris says. "Childish!" Even poolside she wears a gown.

Nell replies, "Betta stop. 'Cause I'm 'bout to throw somethin' back at you."

"Just think," Reggie says, "When summer comes, when it *really* comes, Jupiter is going to boil."

"You get used to it," Polly says. "It's a dry heat. Not a lazy heat. Not like the north."

Nell adds, "It just feels the same old hot to me. Hot is hot, ain't it?"

"Who are those three guys in the yard?" Polly asks.

"They say they're followers. They want to join our church."

"Motherfuckin' stalkers!"

"No," Reggie replies. "They're kind. And they do movies."

"Glamorous," Laurie says.

Polly licks the sweat off her martini. "So, if we're a real church now, do we believe in God? And what's God like anyway?"

Reggie says, "You can believe whatever you want about God, Polly."

"Well," Laurie offers, "if there *is* a God, he's a gay man ... *no*, he's a drag queen."

"God would most certainly have to be a woman," Doris says.

"Well, I was always thinkin' that God was black, you know, since I'm black and all," Nell says.

"Yes," Polly replies. "God is black. A black lesbian."

"Whatever." Doris says. "I've been planning our next party. It's going to be bigger. *Much* bigger. More people. More recipes. More ... *everything*. And in the next cookbook we'll have photos and cocktail recipes and quotes ... and ... I must stop doing cocaine. This will become global if I don't give it a rest."

Nell rises and saddles her basket. "Have to get to goin'. Ya'll be talking about grown up things anyhow."

"Stay for ten more minutes.' Polly says. "You can help with the next party too."

"Can't," Nell says. "Mama ordered me to get home. Says I do too much business."

Reggie grabs her brown arm. "Just five more minutes, Nell. I like having you here."

Elmer Mott wrangles himself from sleep. The ziti supper is tonight. Two hours from now.

He urinates in the sink—belches—calls for Reggie—masturbates—sprays his chest with air freshener. After an hour, Elmer streaks toward the limo.

Doris yells, "Where are you going?"

He races to Barb stinking of pumpkin potpourri.

I know that Elmer is unsure of this evening. But, he enjoys the feeling. Because, after all, it could be simply stellar.

Elmer Mott struts inside the clogged, sleepy Senior Center.

"Follow me," Barb tells him.

Paper chains droop from everywhere: walls, ceiling fans, chair backs. A decayed glitter ball swings above. With so many pieces missing, it looks like a dingy, gap-toothed teen.

"So, what do you want me to do?" He asks Barb.

"Maybe take your hands out of your pockets. Smile. Relax," she says, grinning.

"Okay."

"And please help my friend Clancy visit the buffet."

"Which one's Clancy? They all kind of look the same to me."

"Don't be wise. Clancy is a sweetheart. Just needs a good listener." she says. Barb starts shouting, "Clancy? Clancy? Wave so we can find you."

Elmer spots a senior in a burgundy vest, skidding, dragging, fumbling with his walker.

"Make sure he eats well. Veggies, bread, milk."
"Sure thing. I guess I'm your little helper, huh?"

Elmer says, "All this grub smells pretty good, Clancy."

Clancy scratches the roll of wrinkles on his forehead. "Can I ask you something? Is this a probation thing? Or a rehab thing? Are you some sort of hooligan the authorities sent to take care of us old folks?"

Elmer releases a rif-raf chuckle. "Nope. I'm just a friend of Barb's. Hey, I like your sweater. My favorite color."

"I only wear red. It's a thing."

Someone hacks non-stop. Someone laughs too loud.

Clancy huffs and scowls at the crowd.

Elmer asks, "So … ready to feast?"

"You don't have to be stuck with me. It's okay."

"I spent a long, long time getting unstuck. I ain't stuck with you, Clancy. So, don't you worry. Let's go fill our bellies."

Elmer forked two helpings of ziti onto their paper plates. He also nabbed creamed corn, rolls and pudding.

Anchored beside Clancy, Elmer slops the dinner into his mouth.

"How old are you, anyhow?" Clancy eats only his corn.

"Um … twenty-four. Why?"

"'Cause you got a sauce moustache. You look like some little tyke."

Elmer immediately napkins his face.

"I'm just giving you a hard time. Jesus."

"Well, how old are *you*?"

Clancy swats the air. "Eighty-four. That's no joke."

"Being old can't be so bad. You get free dinners. You guys have dances and bingo and card games and tons of other shit too."

"Sure. We get all that. We also get bedsores, piss ourselves and pay too much for pills. We're all waiting for the end ... instead of the beginning."

Elmer reaches over and nabs Clancy's roll. Tearing at the doughy crust, he pries it apart and smears butters. "So, what do you think of Barb?"

"Everyone likes Barb. And why not? I can tell you do too."

"True," Elmer replies and grins proudly.

"Don't you think she might be on the ... *older* side for you?"

"No, sir."

Clancy smiles. "Tell me what you like about her."

"She's easy on the eyes ... and she's not too sappy. She works so hard ... you know, but for other people. Not herself. Other people are her job. And I don't really have a job."

Clancy unbuttons his vest.

"I wish I could be more like that," Elmer says.

"You could be. We all could be." A streak of discomfort crosses Clancy's face. He grips his torso.

Elmer shrugs. "What? Want some more corn or something? Jesus. I wish they had a bar in here. What about some apple crisp?"

"No. No. I'm fine for now. My meal isn't sitting right."

Elmer fingers the mound of pudding on his plate. He licks the brown dollop.

"I, I think I should go to the little boy's room."

"Need some help?"

"Yeah, and quick."

Immediately, Elmer rises. "It's fine. You're fine. I'm fine. We'll get there before you know it."

Clancy clamps his jaw closed. "Oh, no."

A putrid smell flushes into Elmer's nostrils.

Elmer kicks open the restroom door. A middle-aged man stands at the sink, smoothing his eyebrows.

"Hey!" Elmer shouts. "Fucking leave ... okay?"

The man disappears.

Clancy groans, "I've messed myself again. I'm so ... *embarrassed*. I feel like an infant. A baby." He begins to weep, tears rolling to his lips.

"Everybody shits themselves sometimes. I've done it. It's life."

"How am I gonna clean up?"

"Should I get Barb?"

"No! I'm mortified!"

"I can help, okay? Shit doesn't bother me. Plus, there's a raffle in twenty minutes and we can't skip out on that." Elmer reaches for some toilet paper.

Elmer says, "See. You're fine."

"Can I pay you? Please?"

Elmer drops his smile, turns and peers around the room. "You don't need to pay me."

"A trip to the bar on me, maybe?"

"Won't turn that down." Elmer sees that a flock of seniors have finished their meals. Charred coffee stinks up the air and stiff couples away and dance. He searches for Barb.

Clancy asks, "Will you be at bingo next week?"

"I haven't been invited."

"I'm inviting you," Clancy says. "And I'm telling Barb so."

Elmer spins a foil ashtray with his index finger. He watches it circles like a carousel. "Then I'll be there. Let me see about those raffle tickets. We gotta play to win, right?"

Elmer is slumped, waiting for the coffee procession to move. An Asian woman complains, "They know we like coffee, so make more!" She adjusts her youthful head band.

"Elmer?"

Barb squeezes his arm, but only for a fleeting moment.

"Hey," he says. "Haven't seen you all night."

She grins. "You smell like cinnamon."

"New deodorant."

"It's been one of those evenings. Mr. Knight had a tantrum and they ran out of spoons."

"Oh."

"How is Clancy?" Barb grins.

"Fine. Good. Great."

"Did he eat enough?"

"Yep. For sure enough corn."

"He does have a thing for corn."

"I noticed."

Another soul song begins to thrum bump and grind. Several seniors struggle to their feet.

Barb asks, "Should we dance?"

Elmer is struck with numbness. "Really?"

"I wouldn't ask if I didn't want to."

"Alright, then."

⁂

Elmer cradles her slender back. His hands twitch and tremble. He doesn't want to grip too hard. He doesn't want to embrace too faintly.

Barb says, "Thanks for taking care of Clancy."

"No big deal. He's fun. I like him."

She grabs his chin and forces his focus on her. "No. Thank you for taking care of him. Thank you for taking care of *everything*."

"You're welcome."

"These folks love to gossip. That was mighty big of you. Not a pleasant job, I'm sure."

He smirks. "I don't know what you're talking about, Barb. Easy as pie."

She settles her head on his chest. Elmer feuds with his erection. And new bliss

"I had fun tonight," Elmer says.
"Well, splendid. Me too," Barb replies.
"I'm coming to bingo next week. Will you be here?"
"Of course."

Elmer can feel her lips sliding into a smile through his t-shirt. He pulls her closer, no longer afraid of firm or soft.

I know that Elmer is a little tot at recess.
Careless.
Wandering. Rootless
Free.

There is a rapping on the front door. Reggie thinks that maybe Elmer has misplaced his key, again. He struggles down the stairs, slipping on two steps. Unlocking the door he bears witness to the bulging moon above.

Brad. Or Brian. Or Bret. The Malibu boys.

"Yes?" Reggie asks.

"Can we use your bathroom?" One B replies. "Have to piss again."

Reggie stutters, "Maybe you should think about getting a room in a hotel, or something. You can't live on a person's lawn."

The Malibu boy says, "I guess we should. We're not sure what to do."

Reggie flaps his arms. "Go, go pee. And take a shower if you need. I'm sure there are snacks … somewhere."

Reggie Lauderdale is coiled up in the red room. Too much drink has paralyzed his brain. He strives to not think of ferris wheels, tricycle wheels or anything that spins around. Instead, he floods his brain with calmer scenes. Stretching green acres. Rabbits. Pillows. Huge water barrels.

Serene.

Cool.

F()ine.

Reggie hears coughing and tries to lift his head, but fails. He envisions waterfalls and blankets and clouds.

A weight plummets on the mattress.

"Reggie?"

A Malibu boy arches above him, stinking of sweat and hair gel. Tattooed names climb up his arm. *Mirabel, Bucky, Brock.*

"Reggie?"

"What?" he asks.

"Um ..." he sighs softly. "Me and the guys ... we're really fond of you."

"That's kind."

"We've always wanted to fuck a priest."

Reggie gripes, grouses, groans. "I'm too tired right now."

"Don't worry. You won't have to do anything. You can just lie there. We'll do everything. I mean, there are three of us. We've done it before. For work."

Reggie opens his eyes. He pets the boy's prickled cheeks. "I don't want anyone to see me naked."

The Malibu boy laughs. "You're naked at church all the time."

"That's different. I mean ... *naked,* naked."

Another boy says, "You're fucking beautiful."

"No," Reggie gasps, "I'm afraid ... someone's ruined me."

"Huh?"

"I think ... I'm all ... torn up down there."

"No more than any of the other guys we've fucked, I'm sure."

"I like ... feeling ... like you say ... beautiful."

"Nothing could make you unbeautiful."

Reggie Lauderdale props himself up and laps the boy's mouth like a puppy. In mere minutes, Reggie is shrouded by muscle and moans. All three Malibu boys squeeze up inside him.

Before spurting, one says, "Save me."

And, for Reggie, heaven feels as though it might exist on earth.

Elmer Mott is the youngest person inside the senior center.

"B twelve!" someone hollers. "B twelve. Twelve, Twelve!"

A ceiling of cigarette smoke hovers above. All the the players are locked in concentration, much like prayer. Plywood tables line the room in columns. Elmer sees countless inked up cards and dobbers and over-cooked slabs of pizza and canes and good luck treasures and frowning seniors.

Elmer tips his hat and slides down beside Clancy. "Don't cheat, old friend. You know what they say, 'cheat, cheat, never beat.'"

A gargantuan smile blooms across Clancy's face. "Ah, my new best pal showed up."

Elmer chuckles and lights a cigarette. "You know it, buddy. Won anything, yet?"

"Nope. Never was too charmed when it came to gambling. The ladies ... that's where all my luck came into play."

"Then you're a pretty lucky bastard."

"Now go get yourself a card. Only seventy-five cents."

Elmer swills on his cigarette, the smoke torching his eyes. "I'll just watch for a while. Get the hang of it."

Clancy cackles and coughs. "Lookin' for your girl, Barb, huh?"

"Seen her?"

"Sure."

"We're best buds now. You're supposed to be helping me out."

"Best buds indeed. Maybe I do know a thing or two about Barb. And yes, she asked if you were around."

Elmer hides an oafish grin. "What did she say?"

The caller shouts, "O eighty-eight! O eighty-eight! Eighty-eight!"

Clancy asks, "Do I have that one?"

Elmer squints at the card, eyes rolling over digits. "Not that I can see."

A woman begins to wail, "GOD! Oh my God! Someone help him!"

Elmer looks up.

The caller has crumbled to the floor. He is clutching his chest, pink and wet and shivered. "I'm fine everyone. I'm perfectly fine," He claims.

Clancy says, "That's Gerald. A real dramatic fella. Always puts on productions like this. Better pray that dope Marty Collins doesn't start to call numbers now. He wrestles folk to the floor."

Elmer asks, "Should I do something?"

"No. Well … I wouldn't mind some more orange soda."

And in a split second, Barb stands stood before Elmer.

RECIPE # 98B

There are always endings. To everyone and everything.

But what are endings? I think they are simply new beginnings.

So, don't worry about conclusions, closure. They can't hurt you, really. They are merely beginnings of another trip and another adventure and another chapter and another book.

Reinvention.

Regeneration.

Rebirth.

RECIPE # 105B

Every moment sails on by and I'm guessing you don't realise this until you're old and need to pop many pills. But it's true. Everything happens so quickly. And then it's gone.

So listen. Talk. Pay attention to the people and places that exist around you. Truly try to live … in the moment. It's a full-time task.

Try not to miss out on too much of your life.

Soon, moments will be memories.

"Um ... what's this ball say?" Elmer says. "G sixty-six. Yep. G sixty-six."

Barb pleaded, "Everyone hates Marty and he's already getting revved up. They're only numbers. It's a personal favor ... *to me*." So Elmer trundled to the podium, removed his hat, and began cranking the squealing bingo cage.

"Okay ... G sixty. Anyone got that? G sixty. Yeah?"

Several lift their faces. One gentleman exits.

Elmer feels like a dunce. He is damp. He is dim-witted.

"So someone told me this is a four corners round," Elmer says. "If you get four corners, good for you, but *hear this*, if you get five squares or less, you win two free buffet tickets, courtesy of me. *Okay?* Right then, let's get going."

The crowd brightens and a couple of women lightly clap. One man says, "All fuckin' right then."

Elmer peers at the next sphere. "B twelve! B twelve!"

Elmer realizes he's only got twenty-three minutes to return home for the next party. Spiked with panic, he watches Barb as she shakes hands, rubs backs and eventually cuts through the crowd toward him.

He smiles. "Hi, Barb. Sorry if I fucked up bingo."

She laughs. "No. They loved you. The free coffee and pretzels. Your jokes and your silliness. Not Marty Collins though. He stormed out partway through. A few ladies begged for your return next week. Said it's refreshing to have a nice young man on the podium."

Elmer blanches. "Hey, if they want me back ... I can't disappoint my fans."

"You'd make me really happy ... if you did."

Elmer cannot hide his glow. "You gonna come to *my* party tonight?"

"If I can, then I will."

"It'll be a personal favor ... *to me*."

Climbing the highway, Elmer sniffs cocaine and smokes many cigarettes.

He thinks of fresh trousers.

He wonders about introductions.

He worries about Doris.

He thinks of an anxious Reggie.

He wonders about new followers.

He worries about Polly's mood.

He thinks about nacho chips.

He wonders if he will arrive on time.

He worries that Barb will not arrive.

Reggie feels as though his pumps are welded to the floor. He fumbles with his tender testicle as a flurry of activity charges around him: Polly is stitching a new cape ... Doris is shouting ... The Malibu boys are stringing up streams of Christmas lights ... Nell is braiding her messy hair ... Reverend Rockwell is swerving by a speaker box.

But Reggie could be concrete.

A garden statue.

Reggie calls, "Doris? Um, Doris?"

Doris stops scratching in her notebook and bombs toward him with a hard grimace. "Can I help you, Reggie?"

"Should I, you know, do something?"

"Certainly not. I've handled everything. You should rest. Tonight is going to be enormous. People are calling like mad, even though I never shared our contact details. Also, we made two thousand dollars in donations just from the last party." Her fat eyes are unflinching. "Which is fortunate since we now require these funds. I simply cannot continue inventing glamorous affairs that propel the church." Doris huffs.

"Well, I could do something, if ..."

"Just go and rehearse your recipes. Have some cocaine, but not too much. Try your outfit on …"

Polly skirts by, a muddle of silk and potato chip bags.

Doris continues, "And *you'll* be amazing. *Tonight* will be … amazing. I have ensured it."

Reggie can already feel the disco bass throbbing through the floor. He can smell cigarettes and chicken wings. "I just wish that Elmer was here."

The stage lights die and there is only darkness.
Doris whispers, "Go, go, go."
Reggie tramps down the stairs.
A pop song drips from speakers.
Church-goers yelp, hoot, holler.
Reggie vamps. Shimmies. Slinks.
Reggie sees salad bowls being passed from hand to hand. Crinkled currency mounts.
"I love you!" a guest yells.
Reggie Lauderdale winks and spins daintily, his cape awhirl.
He feels like a medal or a trophy or a first-place ribbon.

Elmer Mott carves through the crowd, edging by pixie-like girls and filthy-faced men. His body gripes with hunger. His body longs for alcohol and powder. But he remains dizzied from thoughts of Barb. He wonders, *Could she like me?* and *Why* wouldn't *she like me?* and *Why* would *she like me?*

"Elmer!" Doris screams.

He drops his head and considers sneaking away.

Doris latches onto his arm. "Where have you been? This party is ludicrous … as you can see. Reggie's already been on and people are asking after you."

"I'm sorry. I was busy."
"With what?"
"Community service, doll."
"Don't be wise." She huffs. "Now mingle and go find Reggie before he has a meltdown. There's a photo shoot ... somewhere."
"I'll give it a whirl."
Doris sweeps a lock of hair from her face. "People here need you, Elmer. Be responsible. It's not just a dumb keg party." She blinks and a shade of sadness drowns her face.
"I need some pizza. And a drink. I'm fucking sorry, Doris," he says, feeling like he just sucker-punched a cancer baby.
Elmer wanders away lost in memory of his slow dance with Barb. He remembers her warm body. Like a quilt in the morning. Like the first summer sun.

A party anthem pumps while Reggie sips his bubblebath. He calls to a plump man, "Do it! Do it!!" And the stranger leaps forward, cannonballing into the pool. Pinwheels of water purl through the air. Reggie spots the silky skyline and believes the sea of stars blink just for him.
"Hello."
Reggie peeps around and sees a buzz-headed boy standing with a pizza box. He towers, all muscle and swollen lips. Veins squiggle up his calves and down his neck. He is an oak. Husky. Rooted. His ears look like jumbo question marks and they are plugged with hearing aids that continue to blink.
"Got a pizza for someone called Alfred." His words lumber, slowly. He speaks as though pebbles litter his mouth.
"I don't know Alfred ... but I'm sure he's here, somewhere.'" Reggie replies. "Just ask around, I guess."
"Oh," he says. "Okay." He half-shrugs.
"I'm sorry," Reggie says, his voice ascending, "I don't mean to be unkind, but are you deaf?"
The boy dunks his head. "Mostly," he says. "Can read lips, though. Can sometimes hear things. I could hear your recipes."

"Really?"

"Yeah. It's nice to hear something so sweet." He sets the pizza box on a lounge chair.

"Thanks. I think I sound dumb."

"You always wear so little?"

Reggie motions toward the party. "For this, yeah. I know it's sort of silly. But it's fun."

"I like it."

"That's nice."

He grins. "You're really something, but I'm guessing you know that already."

Reggie frees a fragile smile.

"A church, huh?" The boy chuckles. "That's what you people call this?"

"That's what they call it."

"Well, what if I wanted to join? What would I have to do?"

A brigade of cameras flash. Reggie swerves toward each lens. "You don't have to do anything. Just … be … you."

"If you come closer, I can better figure out what you're saying."

"Sorry. Okay." Reggie trots forward. "What's your name? You look like a John or a Matthew, maybe."

The boy tugs on his ear. "Clint. Cocker. Clint Cocker."

"That's not a normal boy's name."

"Guess there isn't much about me that's normal."

Reggie can feel his entire body radiate. He is cinematic. "I'm going to kiss you, Clint Cocker. If that won't ruin your life."

Reggie Lauderdale pins himself to the boy. With hooded eyes, he tastes pepper and bubblegum and cheap cigarettes. Clint tongues Reggie's chin.

"Jesus …" Clint says.

Reggie soon tastes iron, salt. Warmth goops over his lips and cheeks.

"Shit," Clint says. "My nose is bleeding. Happens all the time. I'm gonna need a towel."

Reggie hooks onto his jaw. "Don't stop," he says, lapping up rivers of blood.

Elmer stretches beside two snoozing brown girls. He has gathered nacho crumbs and an abandoned screwdriver and he chomps and swills as the Jupiter breeze gently skims his skin.

He listens for Barb's voice, sometimes sweet, sometimes harsh. He looks for her hair, always pulled, always tight. He recalls her scent, sometimes clean, sometimes perfumed, He waits for Barb, always beautiful, always perfect.

Each day, I see that, for Reggie Lauderdale and Elmer Mott, life has bled into a mix of pop religion, glitz and very good deeds. Yes. Both are becoming taxed and worn. But I see them brimming with growth.

The truth is near. True joy is nearer.

Please do read more.

A telephone rings, rings, rings, rings.

Reggie punts Elmer's dozing body. "Wake up, old man. Wake up!"

Elmer jolts and a can of cashews crashes to the floor.

Reggie snorts. "The Girl Scouts are coming soon. Clean up time. There's junk everywhere. You don't even wanna see."

Elmer hacks. "What's that on your cape?"

"A boy bled on me." Reggie shrugs. "He gets nosebleeds. We kissed."

Elmer smiles. "Well, good for you, I suppose."

"You and I, we're like princes here."

"I don't even know what this whole … *thing* … is."

"Maybe it's heaven?"

CHAPTER ELEVEN
WE ARE THE PARADE

"Quiet!" Elmer Mott stirs from sleep to the sound of brawling vacuum cleaners and horse-playing Scouts. He socks a pillow. Kicks the mattress. "Shut the fuck up!" he hollers. They respond with shrill laughter.

The door creaks open. Reggie.

Elmer barks, "Get out, cous. I'm asleep."

"I'll be quick. Promise. Cross my heart, hope to die."

"What then?"

Reggie quickly utters, "The fourth of July parade is on … well, the fourth of July. Only a few days away. I haven't really worn any clothes in a while, but should I wear a bathrobe … even though the whole day is about freedom? Plus, I promised Nell I'd take her to the parade, and Laurie will probably come too. What about Clancy?"

Elmer squints. "Are you high?"

"No … oh, well, a little, I guess."

"Get out, please," he says, tossing over.

"Independence Day is, like, *your* holiday. Stop being such a grouch. You're gonna have fun. Who doesn't love a parade?"

Elmer stretches, moaning. "Goodbye."

RECIPE # 99B

What if life is a long string of mistakes? Foul ups? Mess ups? Screw ups? Are we born to make these mistakes?

Let's say you buy a car, a real jalopy, and it dies in a month. But the mechanic you meet soon becomes your new sweetheart. Let's say you go out for a fancy dinner, candles and all, and later, you're sicker than ever before. But you stay home, get well and gab with you friends all day long.

What if mistakes are meant to be? What if mistakes are gifts, blessings? After all, many mistakes brought me here.

And then, I cooked up all of this.

Giant headphones hug Elmer's ears. A soul track groans and grinds and he allows the crooner's voice to transport him to tender scenes with Barb. Drowsy Sunday mornings. Bingo nights. Ziti dinners. Thrift shop strolls.

Opening his sunburned eyelids he meets Doris hovering above him. A black gown billows from her shoulders down to the floor. The darkest color she has ever donned.

Elmer turns the volume down. "What do you need?"

"I need confirmation that you will be prompt to the party this evening. It looks to be quite the engagement."

"Yeah. I can hardly wait."

Doris looks as though she might actually blink. "Lately, your attitude is deplorable. And rude. You know I love this church. I work very hard."

Elmer rises, fingering his bellybutton. "Well, tonight, I'd rather watch cartoons and eat a calzone."

Doris slits her eyes, "How ungrateful. Honestly, you're a foolish little boy. You don't even know what you're part of." She pivots away.

Elmer claps his hands together and chuckles heartily. "We're all full-time fucking punch lines."

Reggie Lauderdale thrusts through Reverend Rockwell's doorway. An AM frequency crackles.

"Reverend? Hello? Reverend?" He drops a new stack of recipes on the kitchenette counter. "Hello?"

"I'm here." The bathroom door swings opens and Reverend Rockwell appears wearing only his white briefs. His potbelly protrudes, hairless and gleeful. He says, "Reggie. Look at me! I'm adopting your look."

Reggie giggles. "It suits you."

"Well, you're a trendsetter. A real maverick." Reverend Rockwell pops with laughter. "Sometimes you just have to walk around in your undies. That's what I've learned. Want some lunch? Need some flesh on those bones."

Reggie hears a screeching car in the distance. "No lunch today, thanks. I just wanted some ... help with my new recipes. I have so many now that I feel like I'm losing track ... or ... losing my way. I don't know. I just need ... a check up, I guess."

Reverand Rockwell leans against the door casing. "Aaah. You have doubt? The worst sickness of all. Deadly. Reggie, you don't need my guidance any more. You built all these ideas on your own. You built a home with a family of followers. In truth, I should look to you now."

"No." Reggie pets his soft, blonde locks.

"Yes. Of course. Here. Let's give it a try. I've been yearning to ask you ... see ... I'm all by myself. TV can't be my friend. That's why I was so pleased you boys moved in to Dolly and Herb's. But I've been thinking that maybe ... maybe I should start looking for a lady. My wife left me when I quit television and ... since then I've never thought about another woman, but I feel very ... *lonely* sometimes. I don't know if it's okay to find someone else."

Reggie is paved in elation. The man who once governed his thoughts and beliefs is now asking him for counsel.

Reverend Rockwell asks, "So, what do you advise?"

Reggie peers up at the ceiling like a famed starlet. Slowly and carefully, he replies, "I say, friendship and love ... are everything, right? We need each other. We live for each other. Reverend, I know you're full of love. It's bursting out of you. You're one of the most important, special people I've ever met. So, share your specialness. Find a lady. It will be good for you."

Reverend Rockwell remains quiet.

"How was that?"

He cackles. "It was great. And thank you for, Reggie. Now go on. Get going. What if someone sees us like this? A fat old man and a young tyke standing around in their skivvies. What would they say?"

"I don't care what people say, not anymore."

Elmer Mott eyes everything at Jupiter Lanes' Senior Strike Night. The frenzied lasers, the wheelchairs, the scoreboards, the ball bags, the jerseys, the hairnets, the pencils, the clouds of shoe disinfectant.

Clancy asks, "Wanna toss a gutter ball?"

"Naw. Not tonight."

Men topped in newsboy caps nurse flat cola's. Hacking coughs uncoil. Someone gripes about a painful toe.

"You coming here with me is nice," Clancy says. "A chaperone is damn good to have."

"Someone needs to make sure you behave. Plus, I mean, who knows, you could have a bomb in that briefcase you always carry around. You could be a friggin terrorist."

Clancy places the case on his lap and unlatches the lock.

"Is it a box of secrets, Clancy?"

He smirks. "I'm too old for secrets." He opens the case.

Inside, Elmer sees matchbooks, postcards, meal receipts, snapshots, clippings and business cards.

Clancy pulls out a blue cocktail napkin. A smudged date etched in one corner. "Every Sunday, after lunch, my wife and I would spend the rest of the day at our favorite big-time hotel lounge. We had our own special table. We knew all the waiters and bartenders. My wife always had sore toes, so she'd remove her heels and rest her feet in my lap. And we'd stay like that for hours, all the way till closing. Then we'd stumble home and sleep on the couch till Monday morning came calling."

Bowling balls clock nearby.

Elmer smiles, "That's a great story."

"You bet, buddy."

"All that other junk have a story too?"

Clancy glares at Elmer. "It's not junk."

"I get it."

"You don't. There's a whole life in this suitcase. Days, nights, weekends. All the hours I can't get back. But I know they existed. 'Cause I got this suitcase, see. Could you do the same? Could you fill a box with your life, Elmer?"

He looks down at the littered carpet. "No, Clancy. I probably couldn't fill a shirt pocket."

"Maybe that's something to think about."

"No shit."

RECIPE # 112B

When we were small, we would build things each and every day. We'd make castles with beach sand. We'd make spaceships and towers with colored blocks. We'd make pancakes from Play Dough.

The possible creations were countless. We could have built anything!

But isn't this still quite true?

If you think about it for a minute, nothing is impossible. If you use your hands, your voice, your head ... you can construct anything. A family. A playhouse. An empire.

You just need to find your tools.

"Fuck this fucking crowd," Elmer groans.

Drums beat while candy suckers soar through the air. A fire engine wails, a teen queen waves, a synagogue marches.

Elmer tells Reggie, "We should have gotten our own float."

Reggie laughs in his white bathrobe.

Nell, Laurie Fooz and Reverend Rockwell trail both cousins. Human traffic jams the gutters and sidewalks. They are clumsily bumped and jostled in the crowd.

"This is a nightmare," Elmer says. He grabs Reggie's wrist, hustling through a throng of spectators out to the street. They finally emerge beside marching realtors.

"That's better," Elmer says. He wipes his damp upper lip and trudges with the procession.

Reggie says, "I'm dying. I got so used to not wearing much at all that covering up makes me … way too hot."

Nell cheers as Laurie smokes.

"Hey, Clancy's coming tonight. It'll be good for the old fella."

"And Barb?"

Elmer hacks into his hand. "Naw. I think she thinks I'm a dick."

"You're not a dick. Not *all* the time"

Elmer whacks Reggie's shoulder. "*You're* a dick."

"Invite her again. Be formal. Be a gentleman."

Someone tosses three cubes of bubblegum and Elmer scoops them up and crams them into his pocket. He has already collected noisemakers, coins and countless tiny American flags. *For my briefcase*, he thinks, as the loot bulges from his thigh and stabs his flesh. "Gonna read a new recipe tonight?" hHe asks Reggie.

"Yes," Reggie beams. "And I'm almost done writing the new cookbook. I'm just about there. Our second book, Elmer."

A car honks and Elmer flashes his middle finger. "It's *your* book, Reg. *You* wrote it."

"But I wrote it … I wrote them for us. I couldn't have done it without you."

Elmer grins. "Wow. Well, thanks." He chuckles. "Are we boyfriends now?"

"Be quiet. *Dick*. Don't ruin a perfect day."

Elmer sighs. "Don't you sometimes think that everything was simpler before all this? Trips to the arcade. Vic's. Mrs. Lolly. Now we're like …"

"Famous? A little, right?"

"Yeah."

Elmer turns to see a flock of church followers standing by some parking meters. They are pointing, clapping, cheering. Elmer waves.

"Oh my God," Reggie says. "Nell, Laurie, look!"

Elmer waves, waves, waves, waves.

Reggie says, "I thought we were going to *watch* the parade, not *be* the parade."

"I guess we *are* the parade."

I watch the boys march with vigor. I remain delighted.

Dearest Barb,

This isn't a poem, just for your information. I'm no poet.

Haven't really seen you at any of the senior functions lately and I know you're always so busy.

I want to formally invite you to this week's party at the mansion. There will be music, dancing, food and cocktails, of course. Having you there would make it a proper party. So, please come.

You make my insides go alley-oop and loop-de-loop. I hope I see you, Barb, because I'm pretty sure that this will be my last attempt.

Sincerely,

Elmer

I watch the utter rhapsody.

Reggie Lauderdale slinks about, dressed in smiles and little else. Elmer Mott dons a new fedora peeping, scanning for a glimpse of Barb.

Yes. I see it all. Scenesters clogging corners. Mel smoking a cigar. Three brown-skinned boys kissing and pawing in the pool. A wild-eyed Reverend Rockwell. Empty glasses, carpets of drenched confetti, streams of spotlights, the Malibu Boys grinding. A firefighter and two seniors holding hands. A swaying Laurie Fooz. Ribbons and streamers webbing the ceiling. Followers reciting recipes at the bar. A hustling Nell selling heaps of moonshine.

A cyclone of giddy joy.

RECIPE # 129B

It's very important to listen.

During the day, switch off your thoughts, your worries, your visions. Concentrate on listening.. Listen to the world around you. The bring bring of a telephone. A mewing kitty cat. The chatter of mail carriers.

Most importantly, though, listen to the words of others. Pay close attention. Their dilemmas and dreams and hopes should sing in your ears.

This act is true. And kind. And good.

And do not forget to listen to yourself, too.

Elmer hears someone cackle as a new funk tune grooves into life. He stretches on a lounge chair and recalls a time when all he could hear were the power lines humming outside.

Clancy says, "This is one crazy little get together, buddy. Real wild. Can't believe that you and Reggie are so famous."

"Who cares," Elmer sighs, his face souring.

Clancy is clad in his signature red vest. "Gotta get ridda all of your gloom, Elmer. This place here … it should be paradise for a young guy like you."

Elmer scratches his groin. "Did Barb say anything about her coming tonight?"

"Not to me. But don't worry about that now. I'm gonna cheer you up since that's what best friends do. You and me ... let's play a game."

"Let me guess. The hokey pokey? What's that all about anyway? *You're* an old guy. You should know." Elmer is smiling now.

"I'm pretty sure it's about folk getting frisky and foul. But that's not my game. My game is called Gulp."

Elmer fishes an ice cube from his cocktail. He slips it into his mouth, chomps, crunches and minces. "Are we playing for cold hard cash or what?"

"No. Gulp is a game my wife made up. All you got to do is drink some gin. *A lot* of gin."

"Course." Elmer snatches a nearby bottle and swallows the warm, biting liquid. "Did I win yet?"

"Nope. But the first person to fall asleep is the loser."

"We better get a few more bottles."

Reggie Lauderdale feels like a fifty-carat dream. Weaving through his followers he smiles and tosses miniature wink-like waves.

"Want a fancy drink?" Nell's head is cloaked in countless pig-tails and colored elastic bands.

"Not right now."

"You sure?"

"Nell? Don't you ever stop working?"

"In my business, you can't ever stop. Have to work the clients while the clients exist."

Reggie turns, his cape whirling. "You've got to be rich by now."

She shrugs. "Wouldn't say rich. Most of my revenue goes to my mom. But rich *someday*, maybe."

"Well, take a vacation." Reggie crouches down. He stares into her eyes and for the first time notices their sea green shade. "You're a little girl, Nell. You deserve to play. And have fun."

"You sound like a daddy or somethin'." She grazes his cheek. "You don't got no scruff like a daddy, though. Me, I never had one. *You* should be my daddy. I'd be happy about that."

He smiles, "I'd be happy about that too."

"Hello," a warbled voice utters.

Reggie spins around. Clint Cocker. Bright yellow Bermuda shorts cling to his trunk-like legs. He cradles a white carnation inside a clear plastic box.

"What did you bring?" Reggie asks.

"A corsage. For you."

Reggie's face becomes pink. "Well, that's kind, but why?"

"I figured I was supposed to. You know, for a special night." Clint fumbles with the box and frees the flower. "I'm not sure where to pin this. You don't wear clothes."

Reggie locks his hands on his hips.

Clint kneels and carefully pins the flower on Reggie's briefs. He looks up. "Is this okay?"

"Yes."

"I just want to be proper," Clint says. "Do right by you."

"Well, thank you."

※

Elmer Mott is kinked up on the sitting room couch, fighting nausea. He moans and forces air into his lungs, in and out, in and out. A hand begins to gently stroke his back. "Reg?"

"It's Barb."

He squints and sees a shifting sea of swirls. Darting dots of light. In an instant, Elmer shuts his eyelids.

"You look like garbage," she says.

"You came," he drones.

"Wanted to collect Clancy. He's asleep on the patio. People are passed-out all over this place. Empty bottles and trash everywhere. One little girl even offered to sell me liquor."

"Sorry," he mutters.

She sighs. "This is why I avoid you, Elmer."

"What?"

"I'm not a fool. I know about this place. This church. I've heard from Clancy. Others too. It's not for me. Not one bit."

"Most times it's not for me, either. All the hubbub gets me down."

"Then do something about it, Elmer."

"Can you keep rubbing my back please. Just until I'm asleep. Please."

"This is ... ridiculous."

"Maybe I could turn things around. I should run for mayor of Jupiter."

Barb's fingers continue to slowly sow his skin.

"I would put an end to litterbugs. And to cancer too."

※

The telephone has been ringing for fifteen minutes. This nuisance awakens only little Nell.

I watch her scramble and surface from a mess of bath towels. She rubs her dark, swollen eyes and picks up the receiver. "Hello?" she says. And then she replies, "I'm fine, for a tired entrepreneur."

CHAPTER TWELVE
PREACHER BOY FOOL

Today, Elmer Mott will officially debut as the Bingo Flingo master of ceremonies so he skirts through the banquet hall, smiling and kissing spotted hands.

He tells Laurie, "Maybe I should get a hot pretzel before things get rolling? Or maybe not. My gut's stretching out lately."

"You're a stick." She quickly interjects. "Weight is ridiculous anyhow. I met a man who weighed, well, I don't know, three-hundred pounds and he was a real sexy motherfucker."

"Are you ready to become an old folks celebrity?" Clancy asks.

"Ha ha," Elmer mocks, "Remember. You're my ball boy. Just roll that cage and I'll do the rest."

"You'll be fabulous," Laurie says.

Elmer, of course, peers around the concrete hall for sight of Barb.

Clancy asks, "Are you calling full cards first? Or, maybe, four corners?"

"Not sure yet. I'll see what the mood is. See what the bingo spirits say."

Elmer towers at the podium and presses play on a dingy cassette player "Please stand. I mean, if you're able." The national anthem warbles and spits. Elmer places both hands over his chest and mouths each sacred lyric. Partway through, the machine halts. "Fuck," he says, whacking it. The music resumes and plays on until its grand, deluxe finish.

"Take your seats, hold on to your wallets, and get ready to win!"

"I nineteen! I nineteen! Cover your squares folks. I nineteen!"

Elmer becomes a beacon. He shouts. He tap-dances. He sings. He tells knock-knock jokes.

"B nine! B nine! Like a tumor that's benign, folks. B nine!"

Elmer thinks, *I wish Reg could seek me now,*" and *I feel like a fucking prince,* and *I should get a medal for this.*

"Bingo," someone calls.

Elmer squints at the silver-capped heads.

Toward the rear, Barb rises and repeats, "Bingo."

A suspendered man verifies her card, nodding ferociously.

Elmer's face stretches with a jumbo grin. "Well," he says, "congratulations, pretty lady. You just won thirty dollars and a coupon for a free haircut at Mel's Barbershop. Come on up!"

Barb swiftly sidesteps through the throng of players, patting shoulders. Her sneakers appear brighter and whiter today.

"Let's give her a hand!"

The seniors cheer.

Barb reaches the stage, embarrassed and equally amused.

Elmer points at the crowd. "*And* ... young lady, you also win a kiss on the cheek ... from *me.* That's a major jackpot."

Barb leans in and softly whispers, "You're a real prankster, boy."

Elmer hands her two envelopes and smiles. "You win and I win too," he replies. He closes in and presses his lips into her perfumed skin. She is dainty, she is safe, she is strong, she is warm, she is real. 'Now, I'll feel stellar for a week," he says.

Barb shoos Elmer away, but he pecks her once more. "*And now,* I'm good for two weeks."

After lunch, Reggie Lauderdale phoned Clint Cocker and asked him to visit with pizza, tonic and napkins. Now, both boys sit centimeters apart. Reggie's gaze continues to fall on the silver chain that peeks out from beneath Clint's collar. As a

Marilyn Monroe film glows before them, Reggie realizes that he is comfortable with Clint's smell (clean socks, spearmint) and with Clint's voice (busted, topsy-turvy). It is a new kind of comfort.

Reggie taps Clint's shoulder and asks, "Can you read her lips okay?"

He tosses his head side to side. "Sort of. I know she's singing."

"We can turn it off if you're bored."

Clint's entire body puffs up until he finally releases a mega sigh.

"Or we could go for a swim..."

Clint sighs again. "You watch. I have to go to the bathroom anyway."

Three minutes pass. Two more.

Reggie eases into the lavatory.

Clint is urinating. He turns, spraying the toilet rim. "What's wrong?" He asks.

"I have to go too." Reggie replies. He peels down his briefs. "Can we share?"

Clint laughs. "Just don't pee on me."

"I'll be careful." Reggie begins to free his liquids. He watches Clint's chubby penis. Their yellow streams intersect. Crisscrossing, connecting.

"Never tried this before," Clint says.

"It's just whizz," Reggie replies.

"Do you think I'm fun?" Clint asks. "Am I as fun as all your parties and all the party-people?"

"You're *more* fun."

Clint stops urinating. He motions to his delinquent right ear. "Sorry about this. It scares me because I don't want to make things hard for you."

Reggie shakes himself off. "Don't apologize, Clint." He smiles. "I think you're perfect."

"Wow," Clint replies. "No one's ever said that before."

Reggie plunges the toilet lever and their bubbling mess swills away.

Down.

Down.

Down.

I know that Reggie's feet are sore. I know that he draws his gut inward.

Reggie Lauderdale drifts through another mini gala. The party roar is deafening and without reprieve.

Polly's laughter.
Lime wedges.
Crushed Christmas bulbs.
Currents of foul breath.
Autographs.
A drowsy looking Nell.
The Girl Scout cleanup clans.
Faux smiles.
Thoughts of his mother.
Potato chip dust.
Recipes.
Condoms surfing the pool water.

Elmer bolts to his bedroom door.
Elmer ignores the Dolls.
Elmer switches on every box fan.
Elmer imagines Barb, bare, at his side.
Elmer hikes up every blind in the room.
Elmer muscles three fingers inside himself.
Elmer spits on his penis.
Elmer spurts, spotting his beloved American flag.

Reggie watches Clint seep into the room with a rollicking smile. He is naked.

Clint says, "You're so beautiful, I think I could die."

He arches back and replies, "That's awful nice."

Clint moves forward and says, "All I would need to be really, really happy ... would be a life in this room with you. Just lock the door. We could eat and fuck and laugh."

"Really?"

"Yes." His voice creaks. "Yes."

Clint bolts his arms around Reggie, hoisting him onto his trunk-like torso. "I'll take care of you."

"Promise?"

"I promise."

They kiss.

Clint's mouth is slick, robust, kind, searing, slow-moving. And Reggie soaks up each crackle of pleasure. He yanks on his necklace. A silver cross jerks free and Reggie sucks on the dangling charm.

Clint says, "God ... I want to be inside you."

He wakes up.

Semen clogs his briefs.

I can hear Reggie's shrill laughter.

Merry, merry, merry.

In the past thirty-five days, Reggie has regularly kissed Clint's lips and index finger. He has rubbed his prickled skull countless times. He has not, however, held Clint's hand. Reggie cannot curl his fingers around the boy's giant mitts. Instead, whenever possible, he latches onto three or four fingers. Squeezes tight.

I forever see them in this fashion.

Tethered. Boat to land.

Mr. President
1600 Pennsylvania Avenue NW
Washington, DC 20500

Dearest Mr. President,

I hope you're doing okay these days.
I am writing to give you some updates about me. I'm really thinking about making an official change and heading into office like yourself. I mean, it feels good to be there for people and to help them and to give them hope. Don't you think?
I'm wondering what sort of training I would need for my new career goals. Someone told me I should start with a degree in Political Science. That sounds so fucking boring. Shouldn't it just be, if you're nice and honest and mean well, then you're qualified? I think so.
If you could help me out in any way, I would greatly appreciate it. Is there, like, an apprentice program or something in Washington? If so, could you please send me a pamphlet?

Sincerely,

Mr. Elmer Mott

Reggie Lauderdale eyes the crowd, which is dense like dough, thick as a quilt. He waves. Shimmies by a soldier. Poses with three pot-bellied men. As a soul song booms, the Malibu Boys shift by and pinch his rear, sassing, flexing.

Nell pulls on his wrist. "Daddy Priest," she says, "what time is it?"

"Late. *Too* late," Reggie replies.

"Mr. Clint Cocker's been askin' for ya." She motions to the boy who sits on a sofa strewn with littered coats. He is gazing down at his belt buckle.

"He looks miserable," Reggie says.

"For sure." Nell passes him a fancy drink.

He clicks over to Clint. Reggie nabs three of his fingers. "There are so many other places we could be right now." Reggie considers a tree house, or a distant island, or a half-dead motel.

"I've been missing you all night," Clint says.

"Me too."

Clint coughs.

A topless girl patters by, choking on her laughter.

Clint says, "You know, I never thought religion … *a religious house* … would be like this."

"It's too much, I know."

He shakes his head. "It's just different, is all. My grannie, she was religious. She didn't wear heels like you, though. She only autographed checks. Grannie told me and my brothers that the work of God is, like, *a lot* of work. Full-time work. She drove ladies to the store and to their doctor. She babysat. She found money for poor folks and taught them about books and all sorts of things. She cleaned people's kitchens."

I can feel Reggie dulling, dimming.

Clint says, "She stayed up all night while we were asleep and made boxed lunches for folks, just so they'd have something to eat the next day. I don't think she had time for parties…"

Reggie slivers his eyes. "I'm just a silly sideshow."

"No," he says. "No."

"Am I a joke?" Reggie asks, his voice climbing.

"You're angry. I'm ruining your night."

"Clint …" Reggie begins pacing, brawling side to side.

"Should I go?"

Reggie stomps his heels. "No! I thought you wanted a partner. Like a superhero duo?"

Clint says, "I do. I do want that."

"Then you can't leave. If you think something is wrong … you have to tell me. *Tell me*, Clint. What would your grannie say? What would she tell me to do?"

Clint smiles. "It's just like you preach. Be better."

"Okay," Reggie says and huffs. "Better."

Elmer Mott follows Clancy to the entertainment room.

"Where you wanna sit, pal?" Elmer asks.

"Let's see … not too close to the front … and far away from that kook, Jolie Anderson. She's been givin' me the eye. I think she's a bat. A real witch."

Elmer flicks Clancy's shoulder. "You're some heartbreaker, huh?"

Endless rows of clashing, beat-up couches choke the space. The cushions are worn and patched. Four recliners perch nearby, one of which bears a scribbled sign that reads, 'RESERVED.'

Elmer asks, "We should stop by and watch the tube more often. Seems like a nice enough place."

Clancy stops, looks about. "Nah. Not for me. They mostly play stupid game shows or worse, the news. Never did appreciate the news. Only death and violence. It's too sad."

Elmer pluncks down onto a pink, powder-scented sofa. "This is the spot. Seems nice and cozy." He pats the vacant space beside him. "Give it a go, buddy."

Clancy sinks, easing back. "It'll do."

Elmer removes his hat. He thinks, *Where's Barb?* and *I wonder if they'll serve snacks*, and *I should've taken a shit before I left the mansion*.

"What movie are they playing again?" Clancy asks. "Better not be some sob story."

"Sexy Sluts Part Five, I hope."

Clancy chuckles.

"They should give me a room here." Elmer stretches. "How did you end up in an old folks' home anyway?"

"Well, firstly 'cause I'm older than hell. But mostly it's my daughter's work, I suppose. She's a snob. Married some rich-boy banker and … who wants to be bothered by an old fogie like me, right? So, she booked me a room … for the rest of my life. Hey, it's not terrible. It's not prison,"

Elmer kicks off his loafers. "I think this place is pretty nice. I mean, I'd ditch the fucking lasagna for dinner though. Tastes awful. The bathroom floors are sticky too."

"Don't forget the air conditioning."

"And the stench of piss."

Clancy grins. "No place is perfect. You make the best of things. Make your own paradise."

"Ha. You sound like a country song, old friend."

～

The room is dark, threaded with sparse crackles of light. Many seniors have dwindled to sleep while others have escaped to their rooms.

Elmer watches Barb steal by the screen. She grazes a woman's shoulder, squeezes another's leg. Satisfied, she settles onto a flowered love seat.

"Be right back," he tells Clancy.

Elmer hunches down, zig-zags across the room. He whispers apologies to all, awake and otherwise. Creeping over, he collapses beside Barb.

"You must be a new resident, Mayor Mott."

"Maybe." He smiles.

"One might think so. When you're not at a party, you're here with your right-hand man."

"Well, he's one of my best buds."

Barb slips a popcorn nugget into her mouth. "I think it's very kind of you to volunteer for him …"

"I'm not volunteering," he says. "I'm here because he's my friend. My real, true friend."

"I see." Hollywood colors flit across Barb's face.

"Clancy's smart, gives me great advice. He's like my life coach. And … he makes stuff fun."

Barb smiles. "I think that's very, very sweet, Elmer." She inches closer, her body deconstructing as she leans into Elmer's side. At long last, her head settles on his chest.

Elmer Mott is awestruck. This woman, this fortress of a woman, has finally unlocked her gates. Maybe only an inch. But there is a breach. He feels as though Barb is finally seeing who he *truly* is, not just a goofy, dance party, preacher boy fool.

Barb says, "This ain't all we do after hours."

"Tell me more."

Elmer can only hear the ice machine. Retching. Grousing. Wingeing?

"Be very quiet," Barb says.

He studies the corridor, wreaths and knob hangers dressing several closed doors.

"First one to reach the end wins," she says. "On three."

"Okay," Elmer says, hiking up his pants. "I'm ready to kick your ass."

"Please." Barb smirks. "You know how many nights I practice? You're *ready* to lose."

"What is this? The hallway Olympics?"

"One … two … three."

Elmer sprints but Barb shoves him, leaps ahead.

"Fucking cheat!" he whisper-shouts?.

I watch them: stride, pad, stride, pad.

Barb hops over the imaginary finish line, imploding with glee.

"You play dirty," Elmer pants.

"I won. Fair and square. Bet you didn't think I was this much fun."

I hear them heave, breathless.

"What about my prize?" She asks.

Elmer roots through his pockets. Coins clink. "Want a soda?"

"No."

"A chocolate bar?"

"Not right now," Barb says. "I want something else."

They kiss.

And kiss.

And kiss.

And kiss some more.

RECIPE #209B

Someone recently explained to me that real religion, real spirituality ... is work. You cannot just believe in something. You must make it happen.

Church is a place to care for yourself and others. We all need care. I care for you. I'd like to think you care for me too. We should each care for everyone.

There are many, many things you can do.

I'm sure you get the picture.

These recipes, if they mean anything, should be ingredients for a better life. This is, of course, only what I believe. I do hope they help.

So, goodbye.

Thank you.

And bless you.

Reggie asks Reverend Rockwell, "Why do you only have yellow flowers?"

"Well, see, marigolds aren't too fussy. They just grow. You don't have to police them. It's almost like they want to be left alone. They have their own agendas. I like that."

"I think they're pretty."

"Me too, son."

Reggie strolls beside the Reverend, each carrying a jumbo watering can. Splish splish splish. A wet, spotted trail snakes behind them.

The Reverend stoops down to soak more canary-colored blooms. "Doris said something about ... changes."

"I've been thinking, *really* thinking about the church and the cookbook. It's time for something *different*."

Reverand Rockwell swipes his rumpled brow. "Go on."

"There are drinks and drugs, garments and glamour, but there should be more. *Much* more."

"If this is how you feel ..."

"I'm finished with … these books. It's time to start anew."

Reverend Rockwell attempts to flood a flower box, but his well has drained, so Reggie tips his can. A flow gushes over the petals.

"Reggie, do you want to walk away?"

He smiles. "No. What I want is more. More for everyone. That's what this is all about. Right?"

"How would you like to get started?"

"We're having a benefit for the local food pantry. Five cans of food equals one admittance into our next party."

Reverend Rockwell sags, staring into Reggie's eyes. He whispers, "Will there still be cocktails?"

Reggie tweaks with laughter. "Of course."

"Excellent."

Doris drips from the estate clad in a housecoat. She is messed and vamping like a siren. "Reggie," she says, "This new charity venture may be my demise, but it *will* be fabulous, I promise you. I made you more snacks, Reverend."

"Good thing I'm always hungry."

Reggie smiles and says, "I see change is good for everyone."

Reggie speaks, at length, with the dolls about good will and Reggie asks the Boy Scout Clean-Up Crew to flyer all of Jupiter and Reggie purchases a tuxedo at the thrift shop. Reggie speaks, at length, with Nell about starting a more respectable business and Reggie asks Clancy to invite all his friends from the Senior Center and Reggie purchases many thank you cards. Reggie speaks, at length, with Reverend Rockwell about his new aspirations and Reggie tells himself to be better, and Reggie purchases can after can after can.

Clouds of smoke nudge the skyline. A chorus of alarms chime from distant neighborhoods.

Elmer Mott presses a filthy payphone receiver against his ear. He dials and waits, grinning.

"Hello? Who ya callin' fo'?"

"I'm lookin' for a dame ... she goes by the name Lolly." He chuckles. "It's me. Elmer. I miss you like fuck!"

"Who is *this*? Callin' with a nasty tongue?"

There is a pouch of silence.

He clears his throat. "I'm Elmer Mott and ..."

The voice breathes deeply. "Beatrice ... Mrs. Lolly ..."

"Can I talk to her?"

"No, you may not. Beatrice is gone."

"Where'd she go?"

"She passed this week."

"But ..."

"Probably drank herself to death. Sinnin' every day and night."

More sirens howl in the distance.

The woman sighs. "Can I help you?"

"No. I don't believe you can, not now."

※

Reggie Lauderdale is caught in a cage of muscle and flesh. Clint's arms remain bolted around him, unmoving, unlocking.

Still, he stirs. Reggie opens his eyes to see his wet-faced cousin kneeling beside the bed.

"Elmer? What's going on?"

He sniffs. "I don't wanna wake your old man."

"He can't hear anything."

"Oh, right. I always forget."

"Are you okay?"

"I feel sick."

"Do you have a fever?" Reggie asks.

"I just ... hurt, you know ... everywhere. Inside. Outside."

"Let me sit with you for a while."

On the turntable, a record has reached its end. Elmer listens to soft sizzles and snaps. He nestles his head in Reggie's lap. "Don't poke my eye out with your boner."

"Ha. Jerk," Reggie replies.

"It's almost 3:33. Wanna make a wish with me? Memory lane?"

"Okay. Can't hurt."

I see both cousins watch the nearby clock. It ticks, ticks, ticks, ticks, ticks. Two minutes feel like an hour, until the moment arrives, at last.

"Three thirty-three. Go."

"You first," Reggie says.

"Okay. Fine. I wish I could change things. Lots of things. And I wish I could have saved Mrs. Lolly. I wish I could have brought her here to stay with us and Barb and Clancy and everyone else. That was my plan, I think. But I couldn't make it work." Grief flutters down his face. "I wish I could go back in time. That's my wish." Elmer heaves. "Your turn, cous. Time is running out."

"Well … *I* wish *your* wish," he says, smiling.

"Hey, it's a double wish."

CHAPTER THIRTEEN
EXODUS

Confetti guns blow, purging paper chunk squalls. Towers of canned food teeter at every turn. Corn, carrots, beets. Some brought toothpaste and asprin. Others wrote checks. A senior raves in a corner.

Reggie Lauderdale makes his exodus. He sasses up the staircase and through the corridor and by the bathroom and beyond two kissing boys and over a heap of telephone books and, finally, into Dolly and Herb's room. Muscling off his pumps, he places them beside his now famed duos. Reggie spies the party sludge that spots each stem.

To no one but himself, he says, "Tuxedo time."

Each game night Elmer Mott chats to Paulette, a former real estate agent. He carries Bob Henley's bingo bag to his ancient Oldsmobile. He embraces Don Miller. He shakes many, many hands, and winks at women.

Elmer Mott moves at a slower pace. He has learned to breathe slower, talk slower, eat slower.

Right now, he sits, shuffling a scrawny deck of cards. Barb snips and slices crossword puzzles from week-old newspapers.

"I could never do those," Elmer says. "Too hard for my brain."

"Well," she replies, "Hebert can't get enough of them. Though sometimes I think he invents his answers."

"Want some help?"

"No. Thank you."

"Should I make Tessa's night cap soda?" Elmer asks.

Barb peers up, simpering. "*No.* But thank you."

Elmer re-shuffles the cards, which crack, loudly.

Barb says, "You know Elmer, Clancy's napping so you don't have to keep me company."

"I want to."

"Why?"

"Because I do, is all. And you need company, and help, and someone beside you."

"Is that so?"

"You'd never admit it, but yes," Elmer says. "We *all* need someone."

She chuckles, still slicing with steely precision. "So, I need you?"

"Yes. You need *somebody*. Why not me?"

Barb wags the scissors at him. "You and I don't make sense, Elmer."

He glances at the sun-clogged windows. "It doesn't have to make sense. *We* don't have to make sense. Feeling terrific usually doesn't make sense."

Dear God,

Hi there. Sorry it's been so long since we last spoke. I think that you and I just … see things differently. Which is okay. But I know, you know, that you love me. That you want only the best for me. I believe this, truly. So, I'm just asking if you can make sure I do the good I want to. I want to be very good at doing good. Well, thanks a lot. Just so you know, I still love you too.

A satin bowtie cuffs Reggie's neck. He tells a sunglass-toting guest, "You need to bring more food to get in."

The man pats the pockets of his sequined jacket. "Why? We cooking up a feast?" he slurs.

"It's for charity." Reggie proclaims.

"For who?"

"For *charity*. It's a goddamn can drive."

Reggie watches Reverend Rockwell guide the man away.

He turns, volting toward the party. A sweet cyclone of merriment seizes him whole. Elmer croons to Barb on the couch while Clancy scours album stacks. Mel flirts with a middle-aged woman and Laurie Fooz prances up and down the hallway. Nell pours unfancy drinks for several Bingo champs while Doris and Polly embrace by the kitchen doorway.

"Hey. Nice tux." Reverend Rockwell is smiling.

Reggie strokes his cummerbund. "Thanks."

"Already got five full shopping carts for the shelter."

He beams with a royal grin. "Good. Great. Fantastic."

"Pretty soon you can open your very own food bank."

"Maybe one day."

"You could be everyone's daddy priest."

I remark to myself just how perfect Reggie's grin has grown.

Elmer spent close to three hours filling boxes with green beans and black beans and waxed beans. The limo is crammed with buckled-in donations.

Elmer waits, tap, tap, tapping the horn. His boxer shorts are damp with sweat. As Reggie scuttles down the driveway Elmer shouts, "We're full! You're going to have to sit in the front for once."

Elmer Mott sees a new Reggie and thinks, *Hhe is not a boy ... Reg has become a man.*

As palms and storefronts whiz by, Elmer wants to sing a litany of praise. Simply, he tells his cousin, "This would make your mother very happy."

Reggie smiles, peering out the window. "Thank you, Elmer."

Elmer reaches over, squeezes Reggie's wrist and rolls up his window.

Reggie Lauderdale whines, "Jesus." He is stroking himself and sucking his own fingers. "God."

Clint Cocker laps Reggie's scrotum.

"I love how you feel."

Clint stops.

"What? What's wrong?"

He swipes the slaver from his face. "Reggie, there's something in there. What is it?"

"Oh. Sorry. It's like a ball ... on my ball. A lump."

"Oh ..."

"Sorry. It's gross."

"No, it's not. It's just ..." Clints says. "That's not good."

"It doesn't hurt. I'm fine. Don't stop."

Clint rises and kneels amongst the cotton heaps. He fiddles with his hearing aid. "This is serious. You need to see a doctor. *Really.*"

"No."

"I'm worried."

"It doesn't hurt, right now."

Clint rests his head on Reggie's torso and sighs.

Reggie taps him and he peers up. "Don't get upset. That's silly."

Clint rises, his massive hands chopping through the atmosphere. "We need to take care of this. What if something ... happens? I can't love you and I can't marry you and I can't, like, put my babies inside you."

Reggie's cheeks enflame. "That's what you want to do?"

"Yes. Fuck, yes."

"Okay," he says, simpering. "If that's what you want."

Before, Elmer had unfolded card tables. Earlier, Elmer had refilled ketchup bottles, the crimson condiment gooping his fingertips. Minutes ago, Elmer snapped on stage lights.

A retired disco tart, dotted in broaches, twirls and wails on stage.

Elmer Mott squeezes Clancy's shoulder. "Happy birthday, buddy."

"Thank you," he smiles. "Thank you very much, Mayor Mott."

"Got some Salisbury steak on the menu for ya."

"*Ah*. My favorite."

Elmer is grinning so much his cheeks are pink. He gazes around the room and cherishes those who have become his family—his closest. Reggie is nestled with Clint. Reverend Rockwell feasts on dinner rolls while Doris butters more. Polly smokes with Laurie Fooz. Nell colors a card for Clancy as the Malibu boys help her pen the word 'love.' Barb, pristine as always, sits beside a vacant chair.

"Everyone's birthday should feel this good." Clancy says. "Heck. I wish every day felt this good."

"You only get one a year, old man."

"Then maybe I'll start celebrating my half-birthday. Why not?"

Elmer forages beneath the table and finds a gift-wrapped box. "Got you something for being such an old fogey."

"Don't make me get rowdy with you."

Clancy rests the package on his lap and pets the blue metallic paper.

Nell scurries over, beaming like the beautiful child she is. "Ooooh. Can I help you do the rippin'?"

"Of course, sweetheart."

Nell plucks off the bow and slaps it on her chest. Together, they tear away the wrapping. Slivers and scraps float to the floor, shrouding their bouncing shoes. Finally, the gift is revealed; a large, glossy, silver briefcase.

"A new one," Elmer says. "Bigger for more stuff. Its fire proof too."

Clancy smiles. "Hey, you're pretty good at being somebody's best pal."

"True. I *am* pretty wonderful."

"As nice as it is, Elmer, I'd like you to keep it. Start your own collection of trinkets. That would make my birthday even better."

"If that's what you want …"

"It is. And I'm in charge. It's my birthday."

"You got it, boss man."

I ease into the restroom. I adjust my track suit. I see Reggie and Elmer sharing a cigarette. I offer a wave. I search my pockets for coins. I stroke my mangled beard. I purchase a small vial of cologne that costs fifty cents.

"You know the birthday boy?" Elmer asks.

"Of course," I say, "Good ol' Clancy."

"Stop by the table and shoot the shit if you've got a sec."

"I will."

"Haven't seen you around here before," Elmer says.

"Aw. I've met you plenty of times. Reverand Reggie. Mayor Mott."

Reggie inhales. "Have you been to the church?"

"Every service. And every bingo bust. Won every time."

I watch Elmer's eyes narrow. Reggie smiles at the ceiling.

"What's your name?" Elmer asks.

"Gerald. My friends call me Gerry."

Someone flushes a toilet.flush

"Well," Reggie says, "Thanks for coming, Gerry."

"Have a tremendous evening, fellas." I say. "I'll be sure to give your regards to Beatrice."

Elmer balks, "Say what?"

"Mrs. Lolly, of course." I point toward the ceiling. "She sure loves her brandy up there."

I exit, vanishing quickly. I can hear them flop in a fit of laughter.

The moon has folded into the darkness. Orphaned streamers remain trapped in tree limbs, snapping in gales.

Reggie clutches three of Clint's fingers. Alongside Elmer and Barb, they stroll up the stone driveway.

"Clancy had a ball tonight," Reggie says.

"Yeah. Well, I hope so," Elmer says. "He deserves it."

"Reggie Lauderdale!"

Reggie peers up and sees Father Fink hulking beside the fountain. His hair is long and frazzled. Stubble marks his chin. He wears a stain-covered sweatshirt, and like a crime caper criminal, Father Fink is touting a shotgun.

"Reggie! I knew I would find you. Took me some time, but with prayer, I knew we would meet again." He aims the firearm at Reggie.

"Calm down." Elmer shouts. "Stay calm. Just … be calm, Father."

"You ruined everything!"

Reggie cautiously steps closer, "It was an accident … and … I want you to know … I forgive you."

Father Fink cackles toward heaven. "Look at you. Look at all this. Your blasphemous church. Your evil book. Oh, I know all about your new life."

Smiling, Reggie replies, "Isn't it fantastic?"

"It's a joke. You think this is religion? You aren't strong enough to live for the Lord, Reggie."

"I thought the point was to live for each other."

The man begins growling, grunting, wailing, retching.
Bam! Bam! I can smell the heat.
Father Fink's skull implodes. Blood spritzes skyward. Chunks of flesh and bone spatter Reggie's face and neck.
"Praise the Lord," Reggie says.

Elmer wrinkles his nose, watching the champagne tides curl inward. "That's was pretty fucked up. Huh?"
"Um ... yes."
"I thought he was going to kill you."
"Me too, Elmer." Reggie peels off his shoes and socks and grinds his toes into the sand.
"What should we do now?"
"I have an entire list."
"Like what, genius?"
"So much for us to do." Reggie replies. "Go to California. See the doctor. Work harder for the church. Find a new home for the Malibu Boys ... Do you have a list?"
Elmer shrugs. Smiles. "Naw. Just stick by Barb"
"That's as good as anything."
Elmer throws his arms around Reggie. He can feel his cousin clutching fiercely.
Reggie says, "Make me a promise. Every year, you and me will have Christmas Eve dinner at the Pilot's Diner. No matter what. Okay?"
"Absolutely. We gotta try the Number Fifteen Special. Pot Roast."
"Sounds good. I'm adding it to my list."
"This feels strange." Elmer says. "It feels like the end."
"Well, it's not." Reggie replies. "It's only the beginning."

MICHAEL GRAVES

Parade is Michael Graves' first novel. He is the author of the short story collection, Dirty One, a finalist for the Lambda Literary Award in Fiction and an American Library Association Honoree. His fiction has appeared in numerous journals, including Post Road, Pank, Main Street Rag, and others, earning him a Pushcart Prize nomination. Michael is also a contributor to Lambda Book Review. He lives in Massachusetts with his husband.

Visit Michael's official website: www.michaelgravesauthor.com.

Connect with Michael on Facebook: Facebook.com/MichaelGravesAuthor

Follow him on Twitter: @mgravesauthor.

ACKNOWLEDGEMENTS

Thank you to my mother and father for loving me.

Thank you to my brother, Timothy, for being the nicest person in our family.

Thanks you to my sister, Tina, for always being an ancient queen.

Thank you to my mother-in-law, Maureen, for all the love that I love so very much.

Thanks you to brothers-in-law, Steve and Dan, for making me laugh and feel at home.

Thank you to my very good friend, Gregory Collins. I love you, buddy. You're my brother. Our fits of laughter are everything.

Thank you to Kimberly Mooney. You're a darling and I'm grateful for your support.

Thank you to the very gifted Belle Brett for workshopping the baby version of Parade and my other kids on the way.

Thank you to my friend, Jason Anthony. Your wisdom, spirit and talent inspire me! There are so many more magical talks to be had.

Thank you to Laurie Foos, my mentor, my example, my friend.

Thank you to the STORGY Books team, Ross Jeffery and Anthony Self.

A giant heap of appreciation and love must go to Managing Director and Head of Publishing, Tomek Dzido. Tomek, you have believed in me in a way that few have. Your vision and direct guidance has been instrumental in reimagining my novel. Thank you for sharing your genius. Thank you for your friendship. This novel would not be possible without you.

Lastly and with the utmost importance, thank you to my husband, Scott. You're the best part of me, the best part of life. I love you.

ALSO AVAILABLE FROM STORGY BOOKS

THIS RAGGED, WASTREL THING

TOMAS MARCANTONIO

"A beautiful mash-up of grim noir and Japanese flare with a beating heart of motorhead vigilantes. Sons of Anarchy meets Sin City."
– Dan Stubbings –
The Dimension Between Worlds

This Ragged, Wastrel Thing is the first instalment of the Sonaya Nights trilogy; a new dystopian noir series set in the fictional city of Sonaya. Deep in The Rivers, through the winding web of neon alleys, we follow our troubled protagonist, Daganae Kawasaki, as he scours the streets to uncover the truth behind his eleven-year stint in The Heights. But will his search for answers in the dingy basement bars and seedy homework clubs finally distinguish friend from foe, right from wrong, or will he uncover more bitter untruths than ever before? Will he finally find freedom from the pain of his past or will new revelations ignite a lust for revenge? Discover a new voice in modern noir fiction and join Dag on his painful pursuit for salvation and sake.

To discover more about THIS RAGGED, WASTREL THING visit STORGY.COM

ALSO AVAILABLE FROM STORGY BOOK

HOPEFUL MONSTERS

STORIES BY
Roger McKnight

'Hopeful Monsters' is one of the best collections of linked stories I've ever read."
— **Donald Ray Pollock** —
Author of Knockemstiff, Devil All The Time, and The Heavenly Table

Roger McKnight's debut collection depicts individuals hampered by hardship, self-doubt, and societal indifference, who thanks to circumstance or chance, find glimmers of hope in life's more inauspicious moments. Hopeful Monsters is a fictional reflection on Minnesota's people that explores the state's transformation from a homogeneous northern European ethnic enclave to a multi-national American state. Love, loss and longing cross the globe from Somalia and Sweden to Maine and Minnesota, as everyday folk struggle for self-realisation. Idyllic lakesides and scorching city streets provide authentic backdrops for a collection that shines a flickering light on vital global social issues. Read and expect howling winds, both literal and figurative, directed your way by a writer of immense talent.

ALSO AVAILABLE FROM STORGY BOOK

THE DARK STATE TRILOGY BOOK ONE

Featuring the finalists of STORGY Magazines's Annihilation Radiation Short Story Competition the Annihilation Radiation Anthology contains 18 short stories by an array of talented apocalyptic authors. The Annihilation Radiation Anthology explores three era's of atomic annihilation; Before, During, and After. So zip up your hazmat suit and hunker in your bunker with Book One of STORGY'S Dark State Trilogy.

ANNIHILATION RADIATION

To discover more about ANNIHILATION RADIATION visit STORGY.COM

ALSO AVAILABLE FROM STORGY BOOK

YOU ARE NOT ALONE

HELPING PEOPLE AFFECTED BY HOMELESSNESS

With great thanks to contributing authors, artists, and designers, STORGY Books is proud to present You Are Not Alone; An Anthology of Hope and Isolation. Working in close partnership with UK charities The Big Issue Foundation (registered charity number 1049077), Centrepoint (292411), Shelter (263710), and The Bristol Methodist Centre (1150295), You Are Not Alone will help raise funds and provide support for people affected by homelessness following the devastating outbreak of Coronavirus. For far too long the most vulnerable within our communities have suffered in isolation, abandoned and ignored, voiceless.

But we hear our hurting kin; and this is our reply.

You Are Not Alone is an exclusive anthology of short stories and poems featuring a carefully curated cast of international award-winning and emerging authors, including Susmita Bhattacharya, Astra Bloom, Kathy Fish, Tim Lebbon, Toby Litt, Adam Lock, Carmen Marcus, Benjamin Myers, Rahul Raina, Adrian J Walker, and many many more.

To discover more about YOU ARE NOT ALONE visit STORGY.COM

ALSO AVAILABLE FROM STORGY BOOKS

SHALLOW CREEK

This is the tale of a town on the fringes of fear, of ordinary people and everyday objects transformed by terror and madness, a microcosm of the world where nothing is ever quite what it seems. This is a world where the unreal is real, where the familiar and friendly lure and deceive. On the outskirts of civilisation sits this solitary town. Home to the unhinged. Oblivion to outsiders.

Shallow Creek contains twenty-one original horror stories by a chilling cast of contemporary writers, including stories by Sarah Lotz, Richard Thomas, Adrian J Walker, and Aliya Whitely. Told through a series of interconnected narratives, Shallow Creek is an epic anthology that exposes the raw human emotion and heart-pounding thrills at the genre's core.

To discover more about SHALLOW CREEK visit STORGY.COM

STORGY®
BOOKS

We hope you enjoyed
Parade and your excusrion
into STORGY Books.

On behalf of everyone at STORGY - and all
our authors - we would like to thank you for your
invaluable support of independent publishing.

We will forever cherish your belief and backing of
the books we publish.

Thank You!

STORGY®

MAGAZINE

ONLINE ARTS & ENTERTAINMENT MAGAZINE

BOOKS - FILMS - ART - MUSIC
INTERVIEWS - REVIEWS - SHORT STORIES

For more information about STORGY Magazine visit our website.

STORGY

www.storgy.com

@fb.me/morest0rgy   @morestorgy   morestorgy

Lightning Source UK Ltd.
Milton Keynes UK
UKHW011901060121
376538UK00001B/111